MURDER IN THE DESERT

THE PRIVATE INVESTIGATOR ANNIE HUDSON
REAL ESTATE MYSTERY SERIES
BOOK 5

VALERIE BRANDY

EMERALD LION
PRESS

Published by: Emerald Lion Press.

23901 Calabasas Rd., Ste 2088,

Calabasas, CA 91302.

emeraldlionpress@gmail.com

ISBN: 978-1-964161-54-9

Editing provided by Sharon Lennon-Mehlschau.

To request permission to use passages from this book in any context other than a review, please contact the publisher at emeraldlionpress@gmail.com.

Visit the author's website at: www.valeriebrandy.com

🌸 Formatted with Vellum

CONTENTS

CHAPTER ONE

DUST BILLOWED behind the white pick-up truck as it rumbled into Rachel, Nevada. Annie peered out the window, looking at the desert as it unfolded before her. It seemed to stretch on forever, a vast expanse of golden sand and scattered rocks, the heat radiating off the sediment like waves. The sky above was a deep, endless blue, and the rust-colored mountains in the distance only emphasized the fact that Annie and Ethan had driven themselves into a fishbowl. Nevada's desert was the basin of a container, all smooth sides and steep inclines. Annie couldn't help but think of the story of the mouse who fell into a bowl of milk, and paddled so hard in his attempts to escape that he churned it into butter and climbed right out. Annie imagined herself as that mouse, clawing her way up the side of the imposing cliffs that surrounded Nevada's milky desert floor.

They'd arrived early in the morning. Annie checked her watch. It was almost 6 a.m. Just in time for coffee.

She gripped the map in her hands tighter. Hand-drawn red lines— perfected by Fleur's careful artistry— drove them forward. Each crease on the paper map felt like a potential lead, a hidden message that might reveal the location of Russel's compound.

"Any idea where to begin?" Ethan's voice cut through the hum of the truck's engine.

"Not yet," Annie replied without looking his way. Her finger traced a line on the map, pausing at certain points, then pressing down as if willing a clue to materialize. "Fleur and Mark were able to get us to Rachel. Based on the map, it looks like Russel's compound is in this cross-section, less than a mile North of town, out in the middle of the desert. Other than that, we're on our own."

"Might as well be looking for a needle in a haystack," Ethan answered. He kept his eyes on the road. "Russel's compound could be anything. A false business front. An underground facility. Where do we start?"

"With the residents in town," Annie answered. "They'll have seen him before. He stayed here for weeks at a time. He *had* to have stopped in Rachel to refuel and eat. There's nothing else around."

Ethan didn't answer. The silence between them stretched out until it was almost tangible. Finally, Ethan broke it.

"This stop feels different."

"I know," Annie agreed. She didn't have to say why.

"The funny thing about what we've been through is that I don't think about her— Megan— until I do," Ethan said quietly, referencing his sister, who had disappeared long ago. "Think that makes me a bad person?"

"No," Annie shook her head. "I think it makes you a survivor. Listen to me, Ethan," she put a hand on his leg, causing Ethan's eyes to divert from the road. "We're going to *find* that compound. And when we do, we can take down The Collective," Annie told him.

"Doesn't feel that way. Feels like a hunt with no end."

"No. We're close."

"Maybe," Ethan said. Annie could hear a deeper worry in

Ethan's voice, but— for once— chose not to investigate it. "You got Russel's keycard?" Ethan asked.

"Right here." Annie patted the pocket of her pants, the plastic rectangle within pressing against her thigh through the fabric.

"Good. When we find it, we survey what's there, we get what we need, and we get out. Discreet and quick. I don't like it out here. Too remote. Creeps me out."

Usually Annie preferred to be out in the country, but now — presented with an expanse of desert so wide and flat it seemed ready to fold in on itself— Annie agreed. "Discreet and quick," she echoed, thinking about how the desert reminded her of the surface of an alien plant.

The truck slowed as they approached the town's limits, the reality of their mission hitting hard. Small structures provided shelter to the only other humans around for hours. Silence fell again, but it was different now— charged with purpose, with the knowledge that every second brought them closer to the truth.

A sign welcomed them that read:

RACHEL, NEVADA.
Population: 20.

"Twenty people?" Ethan laughed. "Shouldn't be hard to find someone who's met Russel."

"Look again," Annie nodded at a second sign further down the road. It read:

"Home of the Most UFO Sightings in America."

"Maybe the aliens can help us find Russel," Annie said, smiling.

"Can't believe people actually believe aliens are real,"

Ethan shook his head, making a turn.

The truck's tires crunched over the gravel as they officially entered Rachel, Nevada, a scattering of mirage-like buildings welcoming them in. Alien-themed kitsch adorned every corner: a gas station with a UFO crashed into the pump, a motel sign featuring a green figure waving a welcome, and street lamps crowned with flying saucers. Annie took in the strange little town, her eyes wide with wonder.

"Planet Earth to Annie," Ethan quipped, nodding toward a coffee shop with an advertisement for *'Galactic Grub'* emblazoned in neon. "You think they serve little green men on toast here?"

"Only if they come in peace."

Ethan smiled, but it was fleeting, replaced by the furrowed brow of concentration as he navigated through the quiet streets. The town felt deserted, save for a stray dog that watched them pass with disinterest. He sat on his haunches, panting in the heat, the absence of a collar, signaling he belonged to no one in particular.

"Creepy, isn't it?" Annie mused, peering out at the empty sidewalks. "The town's close to Area 51, but nobody seems to stop by for a visit."

"As someone who works for a Government agency myself, I can tell you— the guys working on aircraft at Area 51 don't get off the base," Ethan said. "They're kept in the dark, engineering the next stealth bomber. This town exists for tourists."

"You don't think the crews at Area 51 are working on reverse-engineering flying saucers, then?"

"Of course not," Ethan answered.

They passed an RV Park labeled "National RV," its sign weather-worn and swinging gently in the breeze. A handful of other RVs sat scattered about, lifeless. An American flag hung limp on a pole, and a small inflatable pool seemed like a pitiful attempt at an oasis.

"The RV park," Annie said sharply, her detective instincts kicking in. "My research says it's the only place in town you can get a room."

"Got it," Ethan acknowledged, tapping the steering wheel with his fingers. "National RV Park. Possible point of interest."

"Everything is a possible point of interest," Annie answered, her gaze fixed on the park as they drove past. "Until we find Russel's compound."

"How about that?" Ethan said, nodding down the road at a diner. "Seems like the town restaurant might be a good place to start."

The pick-up truck growled to a halt, dust swirling around its tires. A diner called "Alien Eats" loomed ahead, a beacon of kitsch in the desert heat. A UFO sculpture sat outside to welcome patrons, but it wasn't the sculpture that made Ethan groan. It was the yellow crime tape circling the diner and a parked Sheriff's vehicle, lights flashing.

"Why does trouble always follow us?" Ethan asked. "We should drive away," he said, more to himself than to Annie. "We're on a mission and there's no sense getting involved with something that has nothing to do with us."

"This could have *everything* to do with us," Annie countered, sitting taller in her seat to get a look at the flashing lights on the squad car. "Besides, maybe it's not a murder. Out here, it could be something small, like a robbery or even… an abduction?" Annie smirked at her own joke.

"I'm hoping for an abduction," Ethan said before his face fell. "You don't think 'The Collective' beat us here? That they already found Russel's compound and destroyed it, and whatever's going on in that diner is because of them?"

"There's only one way to find out," Annie said. She opened the truck's passenger-side door, her feet landing on the rocks with a thud. Ethan followed, and the pair approached the crime tape, both of them surprised at the lack of Police presence. There was no fanfare. No descent of cop cars. Instead, the single Sheriff's vehicle sat parked on the asphalt, begging intruders to stay at bay.

"Bet they don't have many law enforcement resources out here," Annie said as she ducked under the crime tape, a grim smile playing on her lips. "You know, for two people who claim to dislike trouble, we always seem to find it."

Ethan grunted, eyes not leaving the diner's shadowed windows. "Trouble's got nothing on you, Hudson. It sees you coming and runs the other way. I just hope— this time— it's not a murder."

CHAPTER TWO

GISELLE

"IT'S A MURDER," Giselle said, her words hanging in the air. "It's not like our victim could have hit *himself* in the head with a frying pan, right?"

Giselle stood rigid inside Alien Eats, her gaze darting from her guests— Annie and Ethan— back to the kitschy wall decor with practiced speed. The diner, usually a homey spot to get coffee, now felt like an alien landscape to Giselle – familiar yet unsettling all at once. Giselle's hand rested on the cool metal of her service weapon, a reflex born from years in uniform.

"If he *had* hit himself in the head with a frying pan, I should think it wouldn't have been a fatal blow," Annie agreed.

Giselle took her hand off her weapon, reminding herself that Annie and Ethan had come in peace. She reached into her pocket removing two items: Ethan's badge and Annie's I.D. She passed both back to their original owners, silencing her radio, its static buzz echoing from a belt loop on her jeans. "Higher-ups cleared you guys. Seems you really are FBI." Her eyes held theirs for a moment, confirming, evaluating. Trust didn't come easy in the desert, but credentials carried weight, even here. "What brought you to Rachel?" Giselle asked. "Funny the two of you already happened to be out this way. No one *ever* just happens to be out this way."

"We're looking for a compound or structure frequented by a man named Russel Grey," Annie said, pulling up a picture of Russel on her phone. She flashed the image in front of Giselle. "Do you recognize him?"

"Never seen him," Giselle shrugged. "Means he must have passed through town without trouble. Only tourists who cause *trouble* end up meeting me. Drunken parties on their way back from Vegas. UFO enthusiasts who think they're going to storm Area 51. That sort of thing. Good tourists rarely cross my path. He must've been one of the good ones."

Annie deflated and tucked the phone into her pocket without a word.

"You don't suppose this murder has anything to do with the man you're looking for?" Giselle asked, trying to seem innocent even though she already knew the answer. *Keep your face neutral*, Giselle thought, trying to control her expression. *Ask the right questions.*

"Too soon to say," Annie shrugged. "Can we see the body?"

Giselle nodded, beckoning for the pair to follow her across the checkerboard floor. Around them, grinning green aliens hung suspended from the star-spangled ceiling, their bobble-heads nodding. They passed a row of booths, making a right to step into the restaurant's back section.

"Over here," Giselle said, leading Annie and Ethan past overturned chairs and scattered menus. A life-size cardboard cutout of a male astronaut loomed beside them, his thumbs-up frozen in time.

A man's body was sprawled near the cash register, a pool of blood surrounding his head. A frying pan lay discarded, its metal surface catching the flicker of overhead fluorescent lights.

"Jamal," Giselle said sadly, shaking her head. "He ran the diner. We've known each other fifteen years," she admitted, her voice trembling. "Can't believe he's gone."

Annie stared down at Jamal's body. He was a man in his senior years, his tightly-coiled, grey hair coated in blood. He wore an apron over his outfit, his arms folded over his chest as if he were still trying to protect himself from the blow that ended his life.

"Who found him?" Ethan asked.

"Me," Giselle admitted. "Found him like this, early today." Giselle's voice betrayed no further tremor, though a vein pulsed at her temple. "I always come for coffee and eggs before my shift starts." She stared down at Jamal, her dark eyes reflecting a galaxy of unspoken thoughts. The jovial man who knew everyone's secrets would serve no more breakfast specials. "Never thought we'd have a murder in Rachel. Things like this just don't happen here. Drunken stupidity— sure. We've had a couple tourists wander into the desert and die from heat exposure. But a cold-blooded murder? Never."

"Any sign of forced entry?" Annie asked.

"The diner door was unlocked when I got here" Giselle answered. "But the diner's always open this time. So that's normal." She shifted her weight from side to side. As the town's Sheriff, Giselle was used to handling petty crimes and disputes between neighbors. Murder was out of her depth.

"Was anyone else here this morning?" Annie asked hopefully.

"Just Allen, but he came because I called him," Giselle answered. "He's Jamal's assistant and he usually works the night shift, so he's gone by morning. He came straight away but he was so upset when he saw the body that I sent him home. Poor kid's a mess."

Annie offered a nod of understanding while Ethan's eyes swept over the blood-stained handle of the frying pan, his jaw tightening. Giselle tracked their expressions, wondering if they found her to be a trustworthy witness.

They shouldn't, she thought, resisting the urge to look away from the pair. *I don't even trust myself anymore.*

"Maybe I shouldn't have done anything," Giselle said nervously, twisting a piece of her long hair around her finger. "I hope I didn't contaminate the scene. I put up the crime scene tape and took photographs while waiting for the bigger team to arrive from Las Vegas, but I wasn't sure what else to do. We learned about this in training— the protocol for a murder— but it was twenty years ago when I was a cadet and I've never seen a murder before. And— and the fact it's Jamal—"

Giselle felt the weight of the room constrict around her, the playful decor now mocking in its permanence. It was too much. The crime scene, the loss of Jamal, the disturbance of their simple life—it pressed down like the desert sun at noon.

Annie and Ethan exchanged a glance. Silent agreement passed between them like a current. Annie stepped forward, her stance solid.

"We'll help you figure out who did this," she said. Her voice didn't waver; it cut through the tension in the room. "If you agree, of course."

Ethan nodded beside her, curt but decisive. Giselle couldn't help but notice that Ethan didn't seem as eager to help as his companion.

The offer hung in the air, a lifeline. Giselle's throat tightened. This was beyond her scope— beyond the quiet routine of Rachel. Pride warred with pragmatism. Her Sheriff's badge felt heavier than ever on her chest. To accept help was to admit a vulnerability, a crack in her armor she seldom allowed anyone to see.

But maybe this would be for the best, Giselle thought to herself. This was an opportunity to bring Jamal justice. And— at the same time— Giselle could stay silent without ever revealing what she knew. It was a risk. But one Giselle was willing to take.

"Fine," she conceded, her tone measured. The muscles in her neck relaxed slightly, betraying relief. "I appreciate it. For Jamal."

Annie gave a brisk nod, and Ethan's lips pressed into a thin line of acknowledgment.

"Where will you stay?" Giselle's gaze shifted from the body to the two agents, businesslike once more.

"Any recommendations?" Annie's brow lifted, waiting. She already suspected the answer, but wanted to verify based on Giselle's response.

"The RV park." Giselle gestured toward the diner's door, the alien stickers gleaming under fluorescent lights. "It's the only place in town. You'll get a roof, but don't expect luxury."

"Sounds like paradise," Ethan remarked dryly. "I just hope it has the same, um," he glanced around the diner, *"alien charm* as the rest of the town."

Giselle laughed. "Oh, don't worry. You'll find the alien thing everywhere. Rachel is a stone's throw from Area 51. Draws in the curious, the believers, and the downright obsessed. Folks here have made peace with the 'strange' and turned it into a commodity. But that's all fantasy. This—" She glanced down at Jamal's body, shivering. "This— is *real*."

After exchanging points of contact and making a plan to cooperate in the investigation, Annie and Ethan headed for the door, stepping out into the stark, Nevada sunlight. Giselle stood framed in the doorway, the alien-themed wind chimes tinkling a soft farewell.

"When you get the RV park, tell Frankie Giselle promised you the best," she called after them. "He owes me one."

Annie gave a curt nod. Ethan raised a hand in acknowledgment before they disappeared around the corner.

Giselle's eyes narrowed as she watched them leave, the diner's door swinging shut behind her with a creak of protest.

Silence enveloped her once more, save for the distant hum of a neon sign flickering outside. Alone now, her thoughts raced.

It wasn't just pride that had made Giselle wary of the Detective's offer to investigate the crime. It was one lingering fact, one truth Giselle had been hiding during the duration of the visit:

She knew exactly how Jamal had died. God, she knew.

The killer's identity was etched into her brain.

She knew who had killed Jamal, but she couldn't tell. Even if it meant breaking her oath to serve and protect. Giselle would take the killer's identity to her grave.

She had accepted their offer to investigate because— deep down— Giselle *wanted* someone to bring justice to Jamal. It just couldn't be *her*. And she worried it would have looked suspicious to decline. With Ethan's contacts at the FBI and their personal interest in the area, they would have gone over her head if she'd claimed she didn't need help with solving Jamal's case.

Now, the best Giselle could do was stay quiet, and never reveal what she knew. Never. She'd never breathe a word. Her secret would remain locked away, buried deep within the shifting sands of Rachel, Nevada.

She could only hope these two detectives weren't so good that they'd dig her secrets up.

CHAPTER THREE

FRANKIE

IN THE SMALL RV park down Rachel's main road, Frankie sat in his office, completely unaware that anything was wrong. The RV park was marked by a tall American flag and a few rows of vehicles that represented the only place to live in town. Sure, a few residents had found lodgings of their own by building homesteads in the sand, but the RV park was home to majority of the population in Rachel. It was also the only hotel in town, and offered a few rental RVs for visitors. Frankie prided himself on being a real businessman who didn't rest on the fact that his RV park was the only place in town to stay. He liked to think he was creating an *experience* for his visitors.

The door to Frankie's office RV swung open with a creak that set Frankie's teeth on edge.

Frankie's office was a used RV that was filled with shelves overflowing with books, papers, and trinkets. The walls were covered with colorful posters and sticky notes, serving as reminders and inspiration for Frankie's work. A small desk was pushed against one wall, cluttered with a laptop, pens, and mugs of coffee. On top of the desk sat a placard Frankie had purchased for himself on the day he inherited the RV park. It read, simply "BOSS MAN." Frankie had worked hard to make this place reflect what he saw himself as— an accomplished business owner. But all the official trimmings in the world couldn't override the musty smell the used RV had come with.

Frankie shielded his eyes from the sun, staring at the open doorway. Standing in the threshold were two figures, casting long shadows over his desk.

"Jamal's dead," Annie announced without preamble, her voice slicing the still air. Ethan loomed behind her.

"Murdered, actually" Ethan added for context. He always tried to soften Annie's abrupt way of imparting news to informants. "We're here to investigate. FBI agent Ethan Beckett and Private Investigator Annie Hudson, at your service." The pair stepped forward, allowing Frankie to get a better look at them. The woman was mousy, but her eyes were bright and clear. The man was tall and fit, but the wrinkles on his face hinted at long hours worked. The man held up a badge. Frankie gulped in response. "Giselle said you might be able to set us up with a place to stay?" Ethan asked.

"Anything for Giselle," Frankie nodded. He blinked, taking in what he had just learned. "When you say Jamal is dead, you don't mean Jamal at Alien Eats?"

"Yes," Annie nodded. "I figured you'd know him, given how small the town is."

"You mean Jamal who runs the *diner*?" Frankie asked again to verify, his mouth dropping open in shock.

"We do," Annie nodded.

Frankie gasped, shaking his head. "I thought— maybe— a tourist—"

"Not a tourist," Annie said.

"So you mean to say, *our* Jamal is… dead?" Frankie shivered, straightening his tie. He wore a tie every day even though the RV park saw limited visitors. Frankie felt it was important— as a businessman— to always put his best foot forward.

"That's exactly right," Annie confirmed.

Frankie's mind reeled. He'd known Jamal for decades and considered him a friend. In fact, Jamal had lived— like so many of Rachel's twenty human residents— right here in the RV park Frankie ran. *Another rent payment, gone,* Frankie lamented. He bit his tongue, glad he hadn't shared the thought aloud.

"That's horrible," Frankie said, doing a frantic calculation as to how this would affect his bottom line. He was grateful to have two short-term guests staying to make up the difference. "Well, if Giselle vouched for you, I'll take good care of 'ya." He tossed the keys to Ethan, who snatched them midair with a nod. Frankie eyed the detectives up and down, wondering how good they were at their jobs and how deep they'd be digging.

Somethin' about them, Frankie thought as he led them out of the RV and into the blistering heat. *They're gonna be trouble.*

The gravel crunched beneath their feet as they wound through the RV park, passing weathered trailers that had seen better days. Frankie rolled up the sleeves of his blazer, puffing his chest out with pride. "I'm an entrepreneur of sorts," Frankie said, smiling. "I take care of this place, and it takes care of me. Rachel might not be much to look at, but out of twenty people that live in town, almost half of them chose to live here!"

"So... ten people?" Ethan asked, unable to keep the fact he was less than impressed out of his voice.

"Nine, now I guess," Frankie shrugged. "Now that Jamal's — you know..."

Annie's eyes darted around, taking in every detail.

"How'd you end up with this place, Frankie?" she asked, her tone deceptively casual.

Frankie's step faltered. This was a question Frankie hated to be asked. One he avoided at all costs. He swallowed hard, giving Annie the answer he always gave when strangers turned up asking questions. "Inherited it from my grandma when she passed," Frankie answered. He kept his eyes forward, but he could feel the weight of Annie's stare.

"Must've been tough," Ethan offered, sympathy lacing his words.

"Yeah, well..." Frankie trailed off, eager to change the subject. "It was. But every day, I work to make her proud. Business is in my blood and I'm one of the top entrepreneurs in this area!"

"No offense, Frankie, but I'm surprised nobody builds houses," Annie said, shaking her head. "The land out here must be pretty affordable."

"Yeah…" Frankie lamented. "But you if you build a house you have to bring in electric, plumbing, and water. Whereas, if you rent from me, these places are ready to go!" He motioned around the RV park. "We got some real nice amenities here. That there's the pool." He gestured to a sad-looking inflatable that leaned beneath in the sun.

Annie raised an eyebrow. "Charming."

"And over there— that's the fire-pit. I added it myself. Ordered it on Amazon and saved for six whole months to get it here. Everyone's real appreciative. Perfect for roastin' marshmallows and stargazing." Frankie pointed to a circle of stones centered around a cast-iron fire pit, ashes still smoldering within. "The stars out here, they're somethin' else. People come to Rachel for the aliens, but they really should stay for the stars."

Ethan chuckled. "You believe in that stuff, Frankie? Aliens?"

Frankie paused, his gaze drifting skyward, imagining the

way it would when night fell. "Sometimes," he admitted quietly, "when I look up there and see all the stars... I do start to wonder. Hard to believe we're alone." He glanced at Annie and Ethan, the closest thing to alien visitors he'd ever seen. "When you two do your investigations, how deep do you dig?"

"We leave no stone unturned," Annie said.

Great, Frankie thought to himself, suddenly very worried that the past was about to catch up with him. *Two nosy detectives poking around. Exactly what I need.*

"Well, then, maybe the two of you will leave believers," Frankie said. Frankie shook off the unsettling thoughts and pointed towards a row of trailers. "That big one there belongs to Sheriff Giselle." He pointed at a massive RV, easily twice the size of any other trailer in the row. It had a sleek design, painted in neutral tones of cream and gray. Large windows lined its sides, reflecting the desert landscape back at itself. A porch had been added off the side, complete with a cabana, providing shade. An elderly woman sat outside, her weathered face creasing into a smile as she waved at them. "That's Giselle's mama, Maria. Moved here all the way from Venezuela to be with her daughter."

Annie nodded, her sharp gaze assessing the woman. "Must be nice to have family close by."

"Sure is," Frankie agreed, a wistful note in his voice. He gestured to his own trailer, a modest affair with a slightly crooked awning. "That's where I hang my hat. Not much to look at, but I'm proud of the changes I made." Frankie nodded at the top of the RV, where he'd built a star-gazing deck. A grill sat beside the vehicle, which had been painted a startling shade of lime green.

Beside Frankie's trailer, a pink Airstream gleamed in the sun. "Now, that beauty belongs to Bianca. She's one of them YouTube influencers, always goin' on about aliens and such. Posts videos about it and everything."

Annie's eyes scanned the Pepto Bismol-colored RV, noticing a logo had been painted on the side in curling black script. The logo read:

Bianca's Beyond: Alien Explorations.

The icon for YouTube and an image of a video camera sat beside the channel title.

"She's got it made up real nice inside," Frankie said. "Usually I rent the actual RVs out, but that one belongs to Bianca and she just pays a monthly fee to park it here. She's travelled all around the country in that thing, checking out the latest alien stories. She's always asking people around here questions."

Ethan's interest piqued. "An influencer, huh? Might be worth talking to her, see if she knows anything about Jamal's murder. Maybe she's seen something on her cameras."

Frankie's stomach clenched at the mention of the crime, but he kept his expression neutral. "Well, she's a bit of an odd duck, but harmless enough." He pointed to the trailer next to Bianca's. It was simple, and due for a wash— dust coated the exterior, and a set of sheets being used as curtains blocked the windows. "That one there is Allen's. He works down at the diner."

Annie's eyes brightened. "Allen? As in, Jamal's assistant?"

Frankie swallowed hard. "Yeah. Allen was really close to Jamal. I'll have to check on him later. See how he is. We all try to stick together around these parts."

Frankie's voice lowered as they passed the trailer next to Allen's. "That's Harlan's place," Frankie muttered. In contrast to Allen's neglected RV, this particular vehicle was downright abused. The bumpers were rusting, its exterior a mess of peeling paint and scattered debris. Beer cans littered the surrounding space, and— as Annie noticed upon closer inspection— the back left tire was nowhere to be found, leaving an empty hole propped up on a wobbling set of bricks.

"Man's a conspiracy nut," Frankie continued. "always going on about government coverups and whatnot. Keeps to himself mostly. I try to get him to clean the place up but he refuses. Would've evicted him by now if it weren't for…"

Frankie stopped himself, his eyes widening as he realized what a terrible mistake he'd almost made.

"If it weren't for what?" Annie asked cheerfully.

"If it weren't for the fact there's so few of us in Rachel," Frankie did his best to cover. "Can't just go evicting someone without all kind of drama."

Finally, Frankie led them to a pristine, white RV, its exterior gleaming in the desert sun. "And here's where you folks will be staying. Nicest one in the park, if I do say so myself."

He fished the key from his pocket and handed it to Annie, his fingers brushing against hers for the briefest of moments. "Well, I'll leave y'all to get settled. If you need anything, you know where to find me."

Annie and Ethan nodded their thanks and disappeared inside the RV. As the door closed behind them, Frankie released a shuddering breath, his shoulders sagging under the weight of his secret.

Just keep it together, he told himself, his heart racing. *Don't give 'em any reason to suspect you and you'll be just fine.*

But as he walked away, Frankie couldn't shake the feeling that his carefully constructed world was about to come crashing down around him. And with Annie and Ethan poking around, it was only a matter of time before the truth came to light.

CHAPTER FOUR

BIANCA

BIANCA SAT in her bubble-gum pink RV, her gaze fixed on the grainy feed of a security camera attached to the home's exterior. A monitor flickered among an array of screens, each casting a pale glow across the interior of her RV, which was a painted a similar shade of pink as the RV's exterior. Stacks of filming equipment were organized in shelves, twinkle lights interwoven between the display. A collapsible chair unfolded underneath a narrow, lofted bed— both splashed with vibrant shades of pink. The RV served as a portable nerve center for Bianca's alien hunting operations, and she'd decorated it so well it looked like it belonged on HGTV. That was part of the game. Being an influencer meant selling a dream, and Bianca liked her home to reflect her status.

Bianca threw a handful of popcorn in her mouth, crunching as she watched a livestream on the monitor. On screen, Frankie's lanky form— shifting under his poorly-fit blazer— guided Annie and Ethan through the RV park. They paused at various trailers, and— from the looks of it— Frankie was offering the strangers a tour.

Bianca tapped her neon-pink fingernails against a compact workstation, watching as Frankie ushered the pair into the empty RV at the end of the line. The door closed behind them, and Bianca noticed a sudden wave of relief washed over Frankie's features as he bid farewell to the duo. Bianca rolled her chair away from the monitor toward the window, lifting up the curtain just enough to take a peek at Frankie, who walked away from the RV with a heavy sigh. Bianca's eyes narrowed, curiosity piqued. She reached for her phone, fingers dancing swiftly over the screen, shooting off a message to Frankie.

BIANCA

Who are they?

A few seconds later, Bianca's phone buzzed. Her fingers, still poised from her last message, snatched it up. Frankie's reply flashed on the screen, blunt and heavy with words she hadn't expected.

FRANKIE

Detectives. Jamal's dead. They think he was murdered. They say they're going to figure out who did it.

Bianca gasped. The RV seemed to contract around her, bubblegum pink walls closing in like a candy-coated trap. She felt her heart hitch, then race. Jamal, the jovial proprietor of Alien Eats, who knew everyone and everything about Rachel, Nevada—gone? It was a surreal revelation, jarring against the kitschy alien decor he so loved.

A memory surfaced, Jamal leaning over the counter, his voice low, words cryptic. "The truth matters more than anything, Bianca." Jamal had been a true believer in alien activity, just like Bianca.

She replayed those words in her head as she spun to her work station, her hands moving with practiced urgency. The monitors blurred to background noise as she focused on one in particular. Bianca had been in Rachel for a few months, and in that time, she'd gathered hundreds of hours of alien-related footage. Fast-forwarding through hours of footage, she searched for a specific moment, that one unguarded moment.

There! On the screen, something flickered—a shadow, a gesture, an anomaly in the night.

"Dammit, Jamal," she whispered to the pixels that held secrets now more vital than ever.

Her fingers flew across the keyboard. Copy. Paste. Transfer. The progress bar filled agonizingly slow, each pixel a countdown to safety or disaster. As the file nestled into the hard drive, she exhaled a sigh that tasted of dust and fear.

With deft movements, she ejected the hard drive and crossed the cramped space to a small safe tucked away under the bed. The door clicked open, the interior dark and cool. She placed the hard drive inside, next to passports and other trinkets of a life spent chasing aliens.

As the safe locked with a definitive thud, she leaned back against the metal frame of her bed. Frankie didn't need to know about this—not yet. Nor did the detectives, with their probing questions and official badges.

"Keep your secrets close," she murmured to herself, the twinkle lights reflecting off her determined gaze. "And your evidence closer."

Bianca crossed to a trunk that was situated at the back of the RV, pulse hammering in her ears as she opened it up. She glanced over her shoulder, half-expecting to see shadows move outside her window. Nothing but the stillness of the desert night.

She flipped the trunk open. Miniature UFO disks, no bigger than coasters, lay nestled in velvet. Fishing wire, nearly invisible against the pink lining, coiled like silver serpents. Her creations, her tools of deception, all crammed into this trunk—the heart of her alien hoax videos.

"Damn it," she hissed. The air felt thin as she snatched a

disk and examined its edges, fingers running across its perfect dome. A prop that might soon become evidence.

Her hand shook. The disk almost slipped from her fingers, but she caught it, setting it back with the others. A bead of sweat traced a line down her temple. *What if these detectives discovered her secret?*

The trunk snapped shut with a thud that sent a shudder through her. Locked again. Her secret hidden away under layers of locks and lies. She couldn't let them find out. Not now. Not when everything was on the line.

"Stay cool, Bianca," she whispered, her voice barely above a murmur, "You've got this."

As she turned away from the trunk, her eyes caught the twinkling lights on the wall. They were supposed to look like stars, a personal galaxy.

Now they felt like eyes, watching her every move.

CHAPTER FIVE

HARLAN

LATER THAT EVENING— in the most run-down RV on the row— Harlan sat on a corduroy brown couch, slamming back a brewski. The glow of the TV screen flickered against his weary eyes, casting long shadows across the cramped interior of his RV. A YouTube video played on the screen, and Harlan leaned in, captivated. This was Harlan's nighttime tradition. Catching up on the day's conspiracies.

On the screen, the man's face spoke straight to the camera, earnest and slightly unhinged as he spoke of cameras in trees, phones listening, satellites tracking. "The thing about the government is that they're everywhere," the man on the screen said, shaking his head. "And today, we've got proof they're listening through your cell phone."

Harlan leaned forward, beard bristling with every nod. They were onto something; he could feel it in his bones.

A sharp rap on the door shattered the quiet conspiracy.

"Who's there?" Despite himself, Harlan jumped. Maybe the government really *was* listening, and they'd come to take him away because he knew too much.

"Frankie," came the muffled reply from outside.

Damnit, Harlan thought. There was nothing worse than a

visit from the landlord. Frankie had probably come with news of some get-together, or another request to fix the state of Harlan's trailer, neither of which interested Harlan.

He muted the video and stood, his legs creaking with the effort. The door whipped open, revealing Frankie's lanky silhouette against the backdrop of desert stars. Frankie's mustache framed his face, and he was wearing a tie, per usual. Harlan didn't know who Frankie thought he was impressing.

"There's detectives in town," Frankie said without preamble, stepping inside as if he'd been invited.

"Detectives?" Harlan's eyebrow arched.

"Jamal's dead."

The words hung heavy, sinking into Harlan's chest like stones. Jamal—always a smile tucked beneath that grey-flecked apron, always a story to tell. They'd become friends over the years. Harlan liked to visit the diner— Alien Eats— and tell Jamal about his latest theories on the world. Jamal had listened patiently and never once made Harlan feel like a crazy person for believing in truths other wouldn't entertain.

"Dead?"

"Listen, Harlan," Frankie leaned in close, the smell of charcoal clinging to his jacket. He must have spent part of the evening cleaning the firepit, still in his blazer. "I came to ask you a favor. Don't get tangled up in your theories over this one. Let the detectives do their job."

"Stay out of it?" Harlan asked, aghast at the idea. "But it's a murder right here in Rachel. A murder of a friend—"

"Exactly." Frankie's gaze was stern but not unkind. "Which is why we should all stay out of it."

"Stay out of it," Harlan repeated, though even as the words left his lips, they tasted like lies. Frankie gave him a final look, part warning, part plea, then stepped back into the night. But before he could get very far, Harlan stopped him.

"I know who did it," Harlan said as Frankie wheeled around. Frankie sighed, visibly biting his tongue.

"No, Harlan, you don't."

Harlan's gaze flickered from the muted screen to Frankie, his mind racing. "It's the woman," he blurted out. "The one I told you about."

"Not this again," Frankie reached a hand to the bridge of his nose, squeezing tight at the space between his eyes. "We've been over this, Harlan. Lots of tourists drive through town—"

"She was in a black SUV with a fake license plate!" Harlan threw his hands up, exasperated that Frankie refused to see the reason in his conviction. "I ran the plates and the number doesn't exist. The windows were tinted. And what tourist would drive around town multiple times a week? Where does she go? What's she hiding?"

"Nothing different than anyone else I'd reckon," Frankie said, shaking his head.

"She's a spook. A government agent visiting Rachel, spying on us all. Jamal believed me and—" Harlan paused, his mouth dropping open. "You don't think…"

"Think what?"

"I told him about the woman, and then a few nights later…" Harlan paused again. "Jamal made me promise not to say, but he saw something, Frankie. Something in the sky the night before he died. Don't you see how it all lines up? The woman. Jamal. The thing he saw. He knew too much and they took him out!"

"Knew what, exactly?" Frankie's question came out more curious than dismissive. "Nobody in this town knows a thing worth killing for."

Harlan paused, wondering if he should betray the trust of his now-deceased friend. Jamal had told him the story over a late-night coffee, and now, after swearing Harlan to secrecy—

he was dead. It occurred to Harlan that— if the government got to him, too— the secret might be lost forever. Harlan took a deep breath. "I'm only telling you in case they kill me," Harlan said. "I don't want the secret dying with me. So… the night before he died…" Harlan paused, swallowed hard, then continued. "Jamal saw a real, honest to God alien ship—a UFO. Over the diner."

"A UFO?" Disbelief tinged Frankie's voice.

"An orb of light," Harlan pressed on. "It hovered real low right in front of the diner windows. Then, whoosh—gone! Faster than anything man-made. It moved in ways no human object could move. Jamal was so shocked he said he dropped a plate. He'd lived here more than a decade never seein' a thing, and then last night— everything changed."

"You're sure Jamal wasn't messing with you?" Frankie asked, dubious.

"No, no, no, it wasn't like that. He was excited as a kid on Christmas morning," Harlan said, the memory vivid in his mind. "He swore me to secrecy because he was going to tell everyone. He was 'gonna get that girl in the pink trailer to help him get his story out there—"

"Bianca?"

"Right. He wanted her to do a story about it with him. He said he thought together they could share the truth and change the world. But now, just a couple nights later he's..."

"Dead," Frankie finished the sentence, the word like a stone dropped in still water.

"Exactly." Harlan's eyes held Frankie's, unblinking. The silence stretched between them, thick with unsaid thoughts and the desert's nocturnal chorus outside. Frustrated by Frankie's lack of response, Harlan began to pace, his mind racing as he put the pieces together. "The woman in the van. The UFO. Jamal's death. It's all connected, don't you see? The government is here in Rachel because they knew the aliens were coming. And Jamal was just in the wrong place at the wrong time." His voice dropped to a conspiratorial whisper, as if the walls themselves might be listening. "The woman in the van must have killed him."

Frankie's mustache twitched with skepticism. "You think she offed Jamal to keep him quiet?"

"Exactly," Harlan affirmed with a nod sharp enough to be a punctuation mark. "Government types, they don't want us knowing about their secrets."

"Harlan," Frankie sighed, raking a hand through his thinning hair. "You're the *only one* who's seen the woman. No one else in town knows what the hell you're talkin' about—"

"Maybe she wants it that way!" Harlan exclaimed, throwing his hands in the air. "But it's the truth."

"Harlan, you gotta let this go. Let the detectives do their job."

"Frankie, I—"

"Nope." Frankie held up a hand, preempting another theory. "I ain't hearin' it."

"Fine." Harlan's reply was clipped, but his mind churned with unvoiced plans.

"Stay out of it," Frankie reiterated, pointing a lanky finger for emphasis before he turned on his heel and strode out into the desert night.

The RV door clicked shut, leaving Harlan alone with the glow of the screen bathing his bearded face in blue light. He watched it flicker before turning the volume back up, allowing the conspiracy theorist's voice to drone on about government surveillance and cover-ups. A smirk tugged at one corner of his mouth.

Stay out of it, he thought to himself, already picturing the morning conversation with the detectives. *Not a chance.*

The desert winds whispered outside, casting eerie shadows against the RV's blinds. But inside, Harlan's resolve was as solid and immovable as the ancient mountains framing the horizon. Tomorrow, he would talk to the detectives. And maybe, just maybe, they'd be the first people in Rachel to ever believe one of his stories.

CHAPTER SIX

ALLEN

IN THE RV next to Harlan's, Allen was still reeling from what had happened this morning at the diner. He had never seen a dead body. And seeing Jamal's body— a man who he'd worked with every day— had rocked him to his core. It had driven home that life was mean. And brutal. The world was a place where only the strong survived.

Allen was in his early thirties— a young man— but most days, he felt like he was in his eighties. Nothing interesting ever happened in Rachel, and he'd worked at the same diner every day of his adult life.

But in the past 24 hours, his world had turned upside down.

Through a slit in the curtains of his quaint RV, Allen's gaze fixed on the scene unfolding outside. His neighbor— Harlan — beard like a bramble bush, gestured wildly with a hand that could double as a bear paw. He was talking to Frankie, who stood outside his RV, nodding with a patience that bordered on saintly.

"Frankie," Harlan was saying, voice just audible through the thin RV walls, "you gotta understand, this woman is from the Government and Jamal saw a UFO. That's all there is to it."

Allen rolled his eyes so hard he feared they might get stuck. He knew the script from here—any minute now, Frankie would pivot the conversation, somehow making the leap from extraterrestrial communication to the state of Harlan's RV. Frankie would— about once a month— ask Harlan to clean it up, but nothing ever improved.

With a flick of the wrist, Allen yanked the curtains shut and sank into his musty armchair. His eyes darted to the diploma hanging lopsidedly on the wall—a testament to an obsolete triumph. *Tech degree, my ass*, Allen thought. Allen had been born poor, and he'd done his best to make something of himself. It had taken him ten years to get through college with a degree in tech, but now that he'd gotten the degree, the tech industry was laying people off left and right. There were few jobs to be found.

Harlan's thrown in the towel on life, Allen mused, scratching at a stain on his jeans. *That's why he never cleans his trailer. Maybe I should stop cleaning mine, too.*

"Life's a glitch," he said aloud, smirking at his own pun. Then his thoughts drifted, like the tumbleweeds outside, toward Jamal. Good ol' Jamal, with his belly laughs and apron flourishes. Unfairness didn't stop that man. It fueled him.

"Miss your UFO pancakes already," Allen whispered, a smile playing on his lips. Jamal had cooked up more than breakfast in that diner; he'd served platefuls of perspective, too.

Allen stood, crossing the room and reaching under the living room table. His fingers grazed the cool metal of a small lockbox. With a quick flick, the latch gave way, the lid popping open with a creak that seemed too loud in the silence of the RV. Allen's eyes narrowed on the contents, his hand snatching a single document emblazoned with Jamal's name.

The paper felt heavy, burdened with more than ink—a last relic from a man who'd made every conspiracy theory sound like gospel. Allen scanned it quickly, his brows knitting together.

"People discounted you, Jamal. They didn't know you were more than just flapjacks and flying saucers," he muttered, stowing the document back into the box. He clicked the lock shut, the sound punctuating his decision to keep this curious find under wraps.

Nobody knew how great you were, except me, Allen thought to himself.

Allen hunched over to his computer, which sat on a desk at the far end of the room. The keyboard clicked as he wrote an email. The subject line read, simply:

"I know."

Allen hoped sending this email would allow him to run the diner in peace and do right by Jamal. With a deep sigh, he hit send, and the computer made a whooshing noise. It was done.

Allen sulked into the kitchen, removing a container of instant noodles from the pantry and filling it with water before popping it in the microwave. There was a clanging sound as the cup rotated in a circle. Allen knew tomorrow would be different. He'd have to open the diner alone, and he wouldn't have time eat before his shift. As he filled a pot with water, the low hum of the desert evening settling around him, Allen allowed himself a small smile. In a world full of mysteries, sometimes the simplest pleasures were the most profound. But he'd better enjoy it now.

He wouldn't be eating noodles for long.

CHAPTER SEVEN

MORNING LIGHT CREPT through a crack between the curtains, casting a soft glow on Annie's face. With a groan, she peeled her eyes open and surveyed the snug interior of their new mobile command center. The RV, though small, was a haven of efficiency, every inch utilized for maximum effect. A lofted bed hovered above the space, accessible by a narrow ladder that they'd ascended with caution last night.

"Another day," Annie muttered, muscles protesting as she slithered out from under the warmth of shared blankets. She threw a leg over the edge of the lofted bed, making her way down the ladder.

"Careful," Ethan murmured, still half in the realm of sleep, his voice a low rumble in the close quarters.

"Always am," she replied, her feet finding the cool vinyl floor.

She sidestepped to the compact kitchenette, filled the pot with water, and scooped ground beans into the machine. The rich aroma of coffee soon filled the space, a familiar comfort against the uncertainty of their case.

"Russel," Ethan said, as if the name itself was a puzzle to solve. "I was thinking about him last night. He's got us all tangled up in another case. Why'd he have to go and die on us?" Ethan sat up, stretching his arms wide as he yawned. "Woulda been a hell of a lot easier if he'd just been polite enough to hang in there until we got the location of his compound."

"Unbelievably rude of him," Annie agreed, pouring two steaming cups of coffee.

There was a thud as Ethan leaped down from the lofted bed, joining Annie on solid ground. They settled into the dinette, knees brushing beneath the table in the cramped but cozy living area. Annie reached into a file she'd left on the table, unfolding the map that Fleur had re-created for them. Beside it, she unfolded a second map that mirrored the first but was slightly different in that it included major landmarks and historical sites in three-dimensional silhouettes.

"Russel's compound is somewhere in this quadrant," Annie said, pointing to an area of vacant desert above the town of Rachel. "Secure. Hidden. Powered. The place has to be far enough away from others that he'd be difficult to find if 'The Collective' came knocking. But is also needs electricity to run computers and tracking equipment."

"If it truly was a command center like we were told, he'd have a tech signature," Ethan agreed. "Russel would have tried to hide it, of course, maybe using topography—"

"Mountains?" Annie suggested, tapping a finger on the rugged outlines of the northern cliffs that bordered the basin.

"Too difficult for one man," Ethan countered, his gaze sharp and calculating. "There might be some caves or carve-outs, but bringing water and power up a grade is a nightmare. There's always the possibility he renovated an existing structure…"

"But the buildings out here are barely passable," Annie said, shaking her head. "Blow on them and they fall over. Not exactly a recipe for security."

"And it's too obvious," Ethan agreed.

"Underground, then?" Annie's mind raced with possibilities.

"Plausible," Ethan conceded. "Doesn't take much to carve out a space beneath the sand. Line it in some metal. You can even get pre-made bomb shelters. Drop one underground. No one's the wiser."

Annie's eyes widened as she stared at the second map, which was dotted with images of the few structures present in the desert. "He didn't need a bomb shelter," Annie said, shaking her head. "Look at this," she pointed at a site on the map that sat a mere twenty-minute drive outside the town of Rachel. "There's a network of abandoned mines out there."

Ethan nodded. "That's good, Annie," he agreed. "An abandoned mine would do it. All Russel had to do was bring in some electricity. Maybe using a generator. Even if he was underground, though, he'd still give off a heat signature, or traces of the technology he used…" Ethan glanced at Annie, a silent exchange of agreement. "We need to call Milo."

"Good idea," Annie said, thinking of their young friend back in Virginia. Milo was a tech genius who lived in a renovated bomb shelter. He could hack anything, from his neighbor's desktop computer to the United States Treasury Department.

Annie's fingers were nimble as she retrieved the burner phone— which had been a gift from Milo— from its hiding spot in the lining of her bag. Annie dialed his number, which she could never forget, even if she'd wanted to. Her perfect memory was a cage that trapped every detail, including phone numbers. The numbers clicked softly in the stillness of the RV. The line crackled to life.

"Annie? That you?" The voice on the other end was distant but not without warmth. "Wild."

"How'd you know?" Annie smiled at the sound of Milo's voice. If she had to guess, she'd say he'd recently taken an edible— maybe one in the form of Gladys' famous brownies — and was high as a kite.

"No one else calls me from an unknown number," Milo answered. "I've got my phone set so even blocked callers will be revealed, except of course, for that burner phone I gave you. I have to say, I outdid myself with that one." He giggled, his laughter higher-pitched than usual. Now, Annie was sure he'd had a brownie.

"Of course you did," Annie said. "Time for your magic, Milo. We need eyes in the sky. I'll text you the coordinates. We're looking for satellite sweeps for heat signatures, or signals from someone using computers in a network of abandoned mines."

"Hey, no problem," Milo answered. "Hacking the satellites is the easy part, but it'll take me a few days to get you an exact location." Annie could already hear keystrokes in the background.

"Understood," Ethan chimed in, taking the phone from Annie. "We're flying blind until we get your intel."

"This is 'gonna be fun. I live for this. But you guys... Dead suspect doesn't help your case, does it?" Milo chuckled darkly.

"Dead ends everywhere," Annie remarked. "We're solving two mysteries at once this time."

"Ha! Two mysteries at once. Classic Hudson," Milo answered. "Stay sharp, both of you. And remember, trust no one. Burner phones only, yeah? Don't go disappearing on me."

"Thanks, Milo. We'll wait for your call," Annie concluded before ending the connection.

The phone clicked shut. Annie traced her finger along the worn edges of the map, its creases deepened by their recent consultations. The RV's small dinette table barely contained the expanse of possibilities spread before them.

"While Milo does his best, let's get back to Jamal," Annie said. "Our second mystery."

"What's your lead, Annie?" Ethan asked.

"I want to talk to all the residents of the RV park. But especially Giselle and Allen," Annie said, images of their faces flooding her mind. "They were the last to see Jamal alive. We'll start there, then move onto the other residents of Rachel. We can ask them about Jamal, and at the same time…"

"Russel sightings?" Ethan asked.

"Same list, double the questions." Annie stood up, stretching her legs, cramped from the confines of the space. "We'll start—"

A knock thundered against the door.

"Right now," Annie said, dejected at the interruption.

"Expecting anyone?" Ethan's eyebrows arched.

"Nothing I expect ever goes to plan, so I stopped expecting a long time ago," Annie winked at him. Then, she strode toward the RV's door, where her hand found the cool metal of the doorknob. She opened it, revealing Harlan.

He stood in the entryway, his hair slicked back, his thick beard giving him the look of a man more at home in the wild than within walls. His eyes, usually lost in theories of government secrets, were now sharpened by urgency.

"Need to talk. About the murder." Harlan's voice was low but insistent.

"And you are… ?" Annie asked, a bright smile on her face.

"Harlan. The one in— the messy RV," Harlan said, pointing at the dilapidated RV parked beside them.

"Ah," Annie said, understanding flickering across her face. "Come in then. Don't think we can decline a visit from a neighbor." Annie stepped aside, allowing Harlan to enter the RV. He shook Ethan's hand, then took a seat at the table, forcing Ethan to wrangle another chair.

"I know who did it," Harlan said, looking at them hopefully. "I know who killed Jamal."

"Well," Ethan said, grinning at Annie. "Thank goodness. For once— we have an easy case."

CHAPTER EIGHT

HARLAN

HARLAN'S HAND SHOOK, the coffee pot's spout clinking against the rim of a mug as he attempted to pour himself another hit. Dark liquid sloshed over the side, a few drops hitting the table with quiet pats. His third cup. Annie watched the jittery bounce of his knee under the laminated wood.

"Maybe ease up on the coffee?" she suggested, eyeing Harlan's restless leg.

"No," Harlan replied too quickly. "I do it all the time. Practically immune to the stuff."

He took a hasty gulp, grimacing as the hot brew scorched his tongue. Setting down the cup, he leaned forward, elbows digging into the table. The urgency in his eyes was palpable.

"So like I was saying," he began, voice barely above a whisper, "I've been seeing this woman everywhere for weeks."

Annie's sharp gaze fixed on him, her mind already dissecting each word. Ethan stood by the kitchenette, arms crossed, demeanor skeptical but attentive.

"Black van. Unmarked." Harlan continued, words

tumbling out of him now. "Tinted windows. But I've seen her face."

"Go on," Annie pressed, her tone cutting through the tension.

"Now," Harlan threw up his hands. "Before you tell me I'm crazy just let me make my case—"

"I don't think you're crazy," Annie answered brightly. A smile played on her lips, and a kind look in her eyes told Harlan she really meant it.

"You— you don't?" Harlan asked, surprised. "I mean, you believe me?"

"Why wouldn't I?" Annie asked, serious. "From what you've said so far, this woman sounds like someone who's coming here for a reason. As a resident of the town of Rachel, you have every right to notice unusual visitors."

"I— I do!" Harlan said, surprised to be taken seriously. He was so used to being dismissed as the local conspiracy theorist that being taken at his word was almost disarming. He felt caught off guard, as if someone had just invited him to a fancy party he'd always long attend, but didn't have an outfit for.

"Now," Annie said, folding her arms on the table. "Where have you seen this woman?"

"Gas station," Harlan said, gesturing vaguely with his hands. "She stopped to fill up. Another time, roadside— phone call. Couldn't hear a thing, but she got out of the car to take the call. Which made me wonder if maybe the van has blocking capabilities. You know, to prevent tracking and the like."

"Anything else?" Annie prodded, leaning closer.

"She's always alone," Harlan added, nodding. "Always in motion."

"Okay," Annie acknowledged, sitting back. "Keep talking."

Harlan's fingers drummed a staccato rhythm on the tabletop, his eyes darting between Annie and Ethan. "She's tall," he started, a faint tremor in his voice betraying the caffeine jitters. "White. Fit. And her hair—it's like...asymmetrical."

"Can you describe it?" Annie asked, her tone encouraging.

"It's short," Harlan complied, shaping his words with pointed gestures. "One side is longer, flops over."

"Her clothes?" Annie pressed on, her mind cataloging details.

"Dark shades. Always." Harlan squinted as if trying to picture the woman more clearly. "Simple. Cargo pants, blank tank top. Phone—like it's glued to her hand."

"Have you seen her inside anywhere? Diner, shops?" Annie queried, eyes narrowing.

"Never." Harlan shook his head. His beard bristled with the motion. "I've seen her fill up the tank and that's it. She never goes inside a business. Never talks to people."

"That's odd." Ethan leaned against the wall, arms folding. "Who skips food?"

Annie's tone was all business now. "Her car. When it leaves town, which direction does it go?"

"North." Harlan's gaze followed an imaginary path. "Every time. Then she vanishes. Hours later, she comes back from the North. Then heads out South. It's the same routine every time."

"And no one else has spoken to her?" Annie's question was sharp, probing for inconsistency. "No locals?"

"No. She's a ghost," Harlan confirmed. "Passes through, leaves no trace."

"Interesting," Annie mused, her brain whirring with possibilities. The pattern. The silence. A piece of the puzzle, waiting to snap into place.

Harlan's leg bounced like a metronome set to a frantic beat. His hand grasped the coffee mug with an intensity that made the porcelain creak. "I think she's involved with Jamal's murder," he blurted, voice low and urgent.

Annie leaned forward, elbows on the table, her face a mask of calculated interest. "Why do you think that?"

"Because," Harlan paused, eyes darting from Annie to Ethan. "There's more. You might not buy it. Because it involves— out there." He gestured toward the RV's ceiling.

"Out there?" Ethan's eyebrow arched, skepticism written in the lines of his forehead.

"Far out." The words tumbled from Harlan's lips. "The night before he died, Jamal told me something secret. Something he couldn't wait to share. Thing is, he'd lived here a long time and never bought into all the alien stuff. But then— the night before he died…" Harlan took a deep breath. "… Jamal saw a UFO."

Ethan's chuckle was muffled behind his hand, but Harlan caught it. An affront. Annie shot Ethan a disapproving look.

"Sore throat, Ethan?" Annie's kick under the table was sharp, a silent reprimand.

Ethan turned the chuckle into a cough. "Allergies," he said to Harlan.

"UFOs are real," Harlan snapped. Frustration edged his voice. "Congress calls them UAPs now. They've had hearings."

"Okay, okay." Ethan held up a hand, peace offering or surrender unclear.

"Jamal was no liar," Harlan pressed on, his conviction a palpable force in the cramped space. "If he said he saw one—"

"Then he did." Annie's agreement was measured, a lifeline thrown into turbulent waters.

"Jamal had all the details. He was able to tell me exactly what it looked like. He said it was an orb that glowed— a golden color— and it hovered real low, just a few feet outside the diner window. It was like it was photographing him. Then, when it saw him watching, it took off at an impossible speed, zooming into the sky." Harlan's gaze pierced through the dim light of the RV, zeroing in on Annie with an intensity that commanded silence. "The woman. She's here for it," he whispered, the words hanging heavy in the air.

"Here for… " Annie's voice was steady, her eyes locked with his.

"The UFO." Harlan's leg stopped bouncing; he leaned closer. "That woman in the black van— she's government. Has to be. She's tracking the UFO and that's why she's been showing up in Rachel the past few weeks. She knew it would be coming here and she was hoping to catch it. But Jamal saw it first. So the woman must have…"

Ethan shifted, uneasy. "Must have what?"

"Jamal saw the UFO." Harlan's voice grew more fervent. "It arrived, and he saw it. She must've found out. Then..." He trailed off, a grim certainty etching into his features.

"Then she killed him," Annie finished for him, her analytical mind processing each word.

"To stop the story from getting out." Harlan nodded, as if his theory was the only possible explanation. "Don't you see how all the pieces fit together? It makes perfect sense."

"But suspicions aren't facts," Ethan said, repeating Annie's favorite line. "Just because the pieces add up doesn't mean the story is true. You need evidence to support the theory."

"That's why we're here," Annie said to Harlan, nodding in agreement. "To get the facts. And everything you've said was very helpful. I promise you, I'm taking it seriously."

"Good." Harlan sat back, spent, his revelation laid bare between them.

Annie stood up, her movements precise, a dance of necessity. "Thank you, Harlan. We've got it from here."

"Sure, sure." Harlan's fingers curled around the empty mug. He left it on the table as he stood, wiping his hands on his pants. "Be careful out there," Harlan warned, stepping out as Annie opened to RV's front door, his boots crunching on the gravel. "That woman? She's dangerous. I can feel it"

"We will." Annie watched as Harlan trotted back toward

his own dilapidated RV, feeling lighter now that he had shared his story with someone who gave him the attention he deserved.

The door closed with a soft click, sealing away the whispers of conspiracy and leaving behind a silence punctuated by thoughts too wild to voice.

"Can you believe that guy?" Ethan said, laughing a little.

Annie looked at him seriously, a concerned expression crossing her face. "Actually… I do."

CHAPTER NINE

ALLEN

ALLEN KNEW what he had to do. He hated that his life had come to this. All he had wanted was to get a great job that took him out of Rachel. He'd earned the degree and looked for work, but still— the jobs had never come. Now, he was stuck here, in a small town with no prospects.

Allen sat in Jamal's office, which was located at the back of the diner. It was a mess, just like the inside of Allen's mind.

The keyboard clicked as Allen typed an email. He'd logged into Jamal's account, and was sending the email as his former boss.

It's going to be okay, he thought to himself. All he had to do was keep his mouth shut.

CHAPTER TEN

BIANCA

IT WAS 9 a.m. when Bianca heard the knock on the door to her RV. She knew it was the two detectives— Annie and Ethan— without even needing to open it. A security camera fashioned to the edge of her trailer provided live-streamed footage to a bank of screens within. The camera was one of many she'd stationed not just in the RV park, but around town, in the hopes of discovering any strange alien life that might increase views on her YouTube channel. So far, the results had been disappointing. Nothing but stray cats and drunk tourists.

Time to play the game, Bianca thought as she stood up from her chair and stretched her arms wide, leisurely making her way to the RV's front door. *Hope these detectives know what they're in for.*

There was a creaking sound as she opened the door, revealing Annie and Ethan.

"Good morning," the woman— Annie— smiled at her. "We're—"

"The detectives," Bianca nodded. "I know." She glanced over her shoulder at the monitors behind her. "I know every-thing around here."

Annie nodded in encouragement as if she agreed with Bianca's high self-assessment. "Then you can help us solve the case, I hope? Jamal, the owner of *Alien Eats* diner has been—"

"Murdered," Bianca answered. "Like I said... I *know*. Come on in."

Bianca stepped aside, allowing Annie and Ethan to enter her high-tech RV. The interior was a cleanly-designed labyrinth of wires, monitors, and computer equipment— all surrounded by pink walls and charming decorations in an influencer-chic aesthetic. A neon sign on the wall read *"Follow your dreams."* Twinkling lights framed the windowsill. The decor wasn't lost on Ethan, who raised an eyebrow as he took in the scene. Annie, meanwhile, remained focused on Bianca.

"So, you have cameras all over town?" Annie asked, her tone a mix of curiosity and suspicion.

Bianca grinned, gesturing to the array of screens. "Yep, wireless ones that feed directly into my command center here. Never know when an alien might show up, and I wanna be the first to catch it on camera."

Annie exchanged a glance with Ethan before turning back to Bianca. "Did your cameras happen to catch anything the morning of Jamal's murder?"

Bianca's heart skipped a beat. *Keep smiling,* she thought to herself. *Don't let them see you sweat.* She knew she had footage, but sharing it would expose her secret. Thinking quickly, she shook her head. "Nah, they were on the fritz that morning. Just my luck, right? But I do have some footage from before the murder."

She plopped into her chair and began typing furiously on her keyboard. The main monitor flickered to life, showing a grainy black and white image of Alien Eats diner. Jamal appeared, unlocking the door and stepping inside.

"See? There he is, going into the diner like any other morning." The door closed behind TV Jamal, who was no longer visible. Then, the footage disappeared, replaced by static.

Annie leaned in closer, studying the screen. "And then what?"

Bianca fast-forwarded the tape, passing hours of blank screen. "Then... nothing. The cameras went out for a few hours. The next thing they caught was Sheriff Giselle pulling up, followed by you two." On the monitor, the image roared to life again. There was Giselle's Sheriff's vehicle. Giselle stood beside it, finishing the work of rolling out the crime scene tape. When the job was done, the video showed her disappearing into the diner. Moments later— Annie and Ethan's white pickup truck arrived.

Bianca could feel Annie's eyes boring into the back of her head, but she kept her gaze fixed on the screen. *Please buy it, please buy it*, she silently pleaded.

Ethan cleared his throat. "That's quite a coincidence, don't you think? Your cameras going out right when the murder happened?"

Bianca shrugged, feigning nonchalance. "Hey, I'm just a struggling YouTuber. I can't afford top-of-the-line equipment. Sometimes things glitch out. Or— "

"Or what?"

"Or maybe someone messed with the feed," Bianca shrugged.

She could tell they weren't entirely convinced, but she had to stick to her story. If they found out her biggest secret, her channel would be ruined. And if they discovered she had evidence of the killer... well, she didn't even want to think about what might happen then.

Annie's brow furrowed as she processed Bianca's explanation. The investigator's instincts told her there was more to the story, but without solid evidence, she had to tread carefully. She decided to shift gears, hoping to uncover a new angle.

"Bianca, did you know that Jamal claimed to have seen a UFO the night before his murder?"

The YouTuber's eyes widened, and her mouth fell open in shock. "Wait, what? So it *was* a UFO?"

Bianca's fingers flew across the keyboard once more, pulling up a different set of footage. "I caught this on camera the night before he died, but I wasn't sure if it was the real deal or just some weird trick of the light."

The screen displayed a dimly lit scene of the diner's exterior. Suddenly, a glowing orb appeared, circling the building before zipping off into the starry sky. Annie and Ethan exchanged surprised glances, but Bianca was too absorbed in her own excitement to notice.

"That explains why he wanted to meet with me," Bianca thought aloud, remembering the email she'd received from Jamal asking to treat her to coffee. When Bianca had come to town, she'd given every one her card and told them to reach out if they saw anything strange. "This changes everything! If Jamal saw it up close, then it had to be a genuine UFO sighting. A *real* one. But now..." Her enthusiasm faded as the grim reality set in. "Now he's gone, and he can't corroborate my footage. It's like the universe is conspiring against me."

Bianca slumped back in her chair, a mixture of frustration and despair etched on her face. Annie sat beside her, offering an understanding look.

"It's hard— to be young," Annie said. "To make something of yourself in a world with so little opportunity. But you should be proud," Annie continued. "I looked at your channel. It seems like you've caught UFOs all over the country."

"But this one was different," Bianca shook her head.

"How?" Annie asked.

Bianca inhaled, realizing she'd gotten ahead of herself. She picked at her pink nail polish, flipping her hair over her shoulder as she considered what to say. "It was different because it's an orb," she shrugged. "Most of the UFO's I've seen so far are saucers or triangles. Enthusiasts say the orbs are the rarest type, and the most other-worldly."

"Enthusiasts?" Ethan laughed. "Of a fake phenomenon?"

Bianca's eyes narrowed as she swiveled in her chair to face Ethan. "Fake? You think this is all fake?" She gestured to the array of monitors, each displaying a different UFO sighting from her extensive collection. "I've dedicated my life to this research, and I can assure you, it's as real as you and me."

She stood up, her petite frame somehow commanding the room. "Let me educate you a bit, Detective. In recent years, the U.S. government has finally started to take this seriously. They even rebranded UFOs as UAPs - Unidentified Aerial Phenomena - to shed the stigma associated with the term 'UFO.'"

Bianca pulled up a video on her main screen. It showed a congressional hearing room, with a panel of high-ranking officials. "This is from the historic congressional hearings on UAPs in 2022. For the first time, the Pentagon confirmed the authenticity of several UAP videos captured by Navy pilots. They showcased objects performing maneuvers that defy our current understanding of physics."

The video played, showing a grainy, black and white image of a peculiar craft darting across the sky at incredible speeds before vanishing in an instant.

Annie leaned forward, her eyes fixed on the screen. "I remember hearing about this. It was a major story."

Bianca nodded enthusiastically. "Exactly! And it's just the tip of the iceberg. There are countless credible witnesses - pilots, astronauts, government officials - who have come forward with their experiences. These pilots are trained to identify our aircrafts, and even *they* say these UAPs couldn't possibly be ours. We don't have anything that can move that way! The evidence is mounting, and it's becoming harder and harder to dismiss."

She turned back to Ethan, her gaze intense. "So, Detective,

before you write off my life's work as a 'fake phenomenon,' maybe consider that there's a lot more to this than meets the eye."

Ethan held up his hands in a conciliatory gesture. "Fair enough. I apologize for being dismissive. It's just... a lot to wrap my head around."

Bianca's posture relaxed slightly, and a small smile played on her lips. "I get it. It's a paradigm shift. But once you open your mind to the possibilities, it's a whole new world."

Annie cleared her throat, steering the conversation back to the case at hand. "Bianca, I know this must be difficult for you, but if you think of anything else—anything at all—that might help us find Jamal's killer, please don't hesitate to reach out. And... one more thing..."

Annie reached into her pocket and pulled out a photo-graph, sliding it across the table towards Bianca. "Do you recognize this man? His name is Russel Grey."

Bianca tore her gaze away from the monitors and studied the picture intently. Furrowed brows and pursed lips. She shook her head. "Sorry, doesn't ring a bell. I've never seen him around here before." She handed the photo back to Annie. "Is he connected to Jamal's murder?"

Annie slipped the picture back into her pocket, her expression unreadable. "We're exploring all possibilities at this point." She exchanged a glance with Ethan, a silent understanding passing between them.

Ethan cleared his throat. "Well, thank you for your time, Bianca. We appreciate your cooperation. If you think of anything else, please don't hesitate to contact us."

Bianca nodded, her attention already drifting back to her screens. "Yeah, sure thing. I'll keep an eye out for any more UFO activity. If the aliens are involved, I'll be the first to know."

Annie and Ethan stepped out of the cramped RV, blinking in the harsh desert sunlight. The door closed behind them with a metallic clang. Bianca let out a deep sigh as soon as the Detectives were out of sight. Her shoulders sagged, her body limp with relief. She glanced at the door, making sure it was securely closed before turning back to her bank of monitors. With a few swift keystrokes, she pulled up the footage of the glowing orb once more.

The ethereal light danced across her face as she leaned in closer, transfixed by the sight. *Jamal saw it in person,* she thought, suddenly deeply upset he wasn't around to validate her footage. The orb was mesmerizing, seeming to pulse with an otherworldly energy. Bianca's heart raced, a mix of excitement and trepidation coursing through her veins. This was it. The moment she had been waiting for her entire life.

She zoomed in on the image, studying every pixel with a keen eye. The orb's surface seemed to shimmer and shift, as if it were alive. *What secrets did you come here with?* she thought, wishing the orb could speak to her.

Her fingers trembled slightly as she reached out, tracing the outline of the orb on the screen. A deep longing filled her chest, a yearning to connect with the alien light. Because— the truth was— in all her travels and in all her videos— this orb was the first *real* alien Bianca had ever managed to capture on film.

Bianca was a fraud.

Of course, she *was* a true believer in the phenomenon. But that was part of the problem. Bianca believed in aliens so much that she wanted everyone else to believe in them too. And— one day— tired of the teasing at from bullies at school — she'd gone and made her own video in the backyard, discovering that she had quite a knack for faking it. She'd uploaded it online and been amazed at the response. Believers from around the world reached out to her. Suddenly, she was a part of a movement.

And she'd craved more.

Today, she was hundreds of videos in, and almost all of

them were fakes. Bianaca had told herself it would all be worth when she finally found the real thing and captured it on camera.

But now that the thing she'd wanted most had happened — her only witness was dead.

Bianca could only hope her YouTube viewers would never find out how deep her betrayal went.

CHAPTER ELEVEN

FRANKIE

FRANKIE SQUINTED through the blinds of his office RV, his lanky figure hunched like a question mark. The dust-coated window offered a grainy view of Annie and Ethan, their figures retreating from Bianca's high-tech sanctum on wheels. The door slammed behind them.

Please don't come here, Frankie thought, waiting. He watched as the two detectives made their way across the RV park, heading toward the parking lot. Frankie exhaled. He'd dodged a bullet. They weren't coming to interview him today.

Still, he thought to himself, *at some point, they'll get to me.*

He turned, the faux leather chair he was sitting in squeaking in protest. His gaze turned to a photograph hanging slightly askew on the wall. There she was—Grandma Dolores, the original RV queen, with a smile wide enough to rival the Nevada horizon. She stood proudly before that hunk of metal and dreams, the first home-on-wheels that rolled onto this patch of nowhere. The RV was a lone landmark in the middle of the desert, unaccompanied by others of its kind. Still, Granda Dolores was unfazed, her excitement spilling over the photo frame. Even then, she knew she'd struck gold.

"Built an empire out of tumbleweeds and starlight," Frankie muttered. He stood and walked toward the wall, adjusting the picture frame. It crooked the other way. "Damn it." Frankie muttered, Grandma Dolores' eyes twinkling back as if in on the joke.

"I won't let you down," he whispered to the photograph, straightening his tie with a flourish that would have made her cackle. He tapped his nose twice, a secret between him and the memory of the woman who could swindle stars into her pocket.

A man's gotta do what he's gotta do, Frankie thought to himself. His pulse hammered in his ears as he glanced out the window one more time. The Detectives were gone. There was no sign of another soul nearby. Certain he was alone, Frankie headed for his trusty old computer, taking a seat at his desk. His hand trembled as he hovered over the keyboard. With a decisive click, he was on the internet, navigating to a design website he'd used to make the RV park's flyers in the past.

"Who needs law school when you've got Wi-Fi?" Frankie quipped to the empty room, a half-smile playing on his lips despite the sweat beading at his brow. He clicked through templates, his gaze snagging on one that looked official. "Bingo," he said, and began the dance of drag-and-drop.

Minutes ticked by, filled only with the clatter of keys and Frankie's muttered incantations to tech gods. Then, a printer in the corner of the RV whirred to life, coughing out his salvation sheet by sheet. Frankie leapt up, snatched the papers, and inspected his handiwork— multiple copies of a land deed looked back at him. Each one contained a state seal and looping cursive typography, but the layouts were slightly different. Frankie paused, sorting through the copies, selecting the one he though looked the most authentic.

When he'd found it, he pulled it from the stack, thinking all the while that Grandma Dolores would have been proud of what he'd done. She'd never believed in aliens— but she'e believed in the promise of the town of Rachel.

Frankie sighed, tucking the chosen false land deed into a folder labeled "DOCUMENTS." Although Frankie thought of himself as a business man and liked all the trappings that came with it— a desk, a filing cabinet, his collection of ties— he secretly often felt that he had no idea what he was doing. He imagined himself as a kid with a crayon trying to manage an estate. Insurance policies. Rent kept in trust. Frankie knew there were things he was supposed to be doing to run a legal operation. But, for the most part, he just took people's money and put it in the bank, and then waited until next month to do it again.

Frankie had never been good at details.

Frankie ran a hand over his blazer, straightening it out of habit. He took a deep breath and steeled himself, knowing one day those Detectives would knock on his door and want to know everything. But when they came, he'd be ready.

He glanced down at his tie, willing himself to be the kind of man that was worthy of it. "Let 'em come," he whispered to himself. "I've got this covered."

CHAPTER TWELVE

GISELLE

GISELLE DRUMMED her fingers on the sticky surface of the diner's formica table, the rhythmic tap-tap-tap echoing in the quiet hum of Alien Eats. Her Sheriff's uniform felt especially tight against her skin today, almost as if it had shrunk in the wash. A cup of coffee sat before her, half-empty, tendrils of steam mingling with the scent of grease that clung to the air. This place had been like a second home to her. In-between patrolling the town of Rachel, she would pop by for some banter with Jamal, or one of the diner's famous breakfast burritos. But not anymore. Now, the diner felt foreign. Like a place she'd been to once long ago, and would rather forget.

Giselle's gaze flicked to the phone nestled beside her hand, its screen illuminated by a message bubble:

ANNIE

Meet at Alien Eats? We have an update on the case.

GISELLE

Sure. See you there. 10 a.m.

Giselle glanced at the time on her phone screen. It was now 10:03.

The diner hadn't been Giselle's first choice for a meeting spot— but since Annie had suggested it, she'd agreed. She didn't want to arouse Annie's suspicion by suggesting another location.

"Waiting for someone?" Allen's voice cut through Giselle's reverie as he approached with a coffee pot in hand, a look of sympathy etched across his face.

Giselle stared up at him, feeling as if she'd been caught. It was better, she decided, to tell the truth. "The Detectives asked to meet with me," she said, shaking her head. "Could hardly say no."

"They're late, aren't they?" Allen quipped, topping off the mug of coffee Giselle was holding. The liquid sloshed precariously close to the rim. Giselle's hand trembled. She hoped Allen didn't notice.

"Guess they'll show when they feel like it," Giselle answered.

"You're the Sheriff in town. You've got all the power." Allen's tone held an edge of irony, not lost on Giselle. Power seemed like a cruel joke when you were out of your depth.

"Doesn't seem that way," Giselle answered, wrapping her hands around the warm ceramic mug.

Allen leaned in closer, his voice dipping to a conspiratorial whisper. "I wouldn't mention your Mom. We don't know where they stand on these kinds of things. Opinions are mixed right now."

"Thanks for the pep talk, Allen," Giselle said, her smile tight and final. Giselle's mother was in the country without the proper paperwork. And while Allen's point was well taken— she hoped he would leave.

Thankfully, the bell above the door jingled, announcing the arrival of her expected company.

Annie and Ethan slid into the booth across from Giselle,

bringing with them a blast of desert heat that momentarily warred with the diner's overzealous air conditioning.

"Space burgers on the way," Giselle said, jabbing a thumb at the menu's star attraction. "Figured we could all use a taste of the cosmos."

"Appreciate it," Annie replied, her eyes scanning the kitsch décor with a pleasant arch of an eyebrow.

"Alien cuisine? I've been briefed on what do in case of a terrorist attack, but *this* wasn't covered at Quantico," Ethan quipped, easing the tension with a smirk.

"Consider it local flavor," Giselle shot back. Her humor was dry, but there was no hiding the flicker of amusement in her eyes. For a moment, she thought about Jamal and remembered the hours he'd spent furbishing the diner in alien-themed decorations. Images of Jamal— up on a ladder, a fake UFO in hand— back in the kitchen, using food dye to make the hamburger buns green— smiling as he opened the doors — flashed before her eyes. She pushed them away. Giselle wanted to do right by Jamal, but he was gone now. All that was left was taking care of her own mess.

Annie leaned forward, elbows bracing against the sticky tabletop. "Giselle, you're the town's pulse. Did Jamal have any enemies?"

"Enemies?" Giselle snorted. "The man couldn't find an enemy anywhere. He was loved by all. Wouldn't pick a fight to save his life. He was a turn the other cheek type of guy,"

"Friends, then?" Annie pressed, her gaze sharp.

"Jamal had more friends than this place has flying saucers," Giselle declared, gesturing to the ceiling where plastic UFOs dangled precariously. "He was Rachel's unofficial welcome wagon. There's not many other places to eat in town, so everyone who comes through stops here first. For tourists it's a fun experience. For locals, it's our watering hole. Jamal was the center of it all. Always a smile if you'd had a hard day. A free cup of coffee when the weather turned sour.

Jamal knew he mattered to the town, and he gave back as much as he got."

"Must have been quite the guy," Ethan murmured, his voice low and respectful.

"Best damn burger flipper in the galaxy," Giselle confirmed, a wistful note creeping into her tone. "He made this place feel like home for all of us. We don't have a lot of services in Rachel, if you hadn't noticed. Nearest drug store is an hour away. A place like this? It means a lot. He could have opened it somewhere else where he'd have had more foot traffic, but Jamal believed in Rachel."

"Did he believe in UFOs, too?" Annie asked.

The clink of ceramic on formica cut through the murmur of conversation as Giselle set her coffee cup down. Her gaze flicked back to Annie, whose question seemed to hang in the air, invisible and yet palpable.

"UFOs?" Giselle's eyes crinkled in suspicion. She motioned around the diner. "It's a tourist trap. Not a declaration."

"Did Jamal ever mention *seeing* a UFO?" Annie prodded.

"I—" Giselle's hand froze mid-air, knuckles whitening around the mug handle. "Jamal thought those stories were just spice for the tourists. He thought they were a kind of group hallucination. We talked about it late one night, when I was getting off a shift." Giselle's eyes darted to her coffee mug as the memory played back in her mind. "He said UFOs were a symbol of believing in something bigger than yourself. And— even though he thought they weren't real— he liked that it gave people something to rally around. And he *loved* what it meant for the town. Without UFOs, Rachel would be nothing."

"Interesting," Annie said, tapping a finger against her lips. "If he saw something, that changes the narrative."

"Saw something?" Giselle murmured, her curiosity piqued. "When?"

"The night before he died, Jamal saw a UFO. He told Harlan about it. Harlan thinks it led to his death."

Giselle waved a hand in the air. "That doesn't sound like Jamal. And Harlan's full of stories—"

"It *would* take a lot to make a non-believer change his mind," Annie agreed. "But what Jamal saw was quite riveting. Bianca got it on video," Annie added. "She showed us the tape. It was a giant glowing orb that hovered right by that window—" Annie pointed at the window two booths over to make her point.

"How— that's not possible." Giselle said. "It had to be a drone. Or a trick of the light."

"She's got cameras all over town," Ethan said. "Some kind of fancy technology using Starlink. They're all sending video back to Giselle's computer in the hopes she catches a UFO." He nodded out the window next to the booth, pointing at a lamppost in the parking lot. "See the camera, right there?"

Giselle leaned forward, just barely able to make out a tiny, white camera strapped to the top of the lamppost in the parking lot. She never would have spotted it if Ethan hadn't pointed it out. She wondered how many others were around town, and more importantly, how long they'd been there.

Giselle's face blanched. *What else did Bianca get on video?* she wondered, heart pounding.

"Unfortunately"," Annie continued, seeming to read Giselle's mind, "She didn't manage to get the murder on tape. Bit of a shame, isn't it?"

Giselle couldn't help it. She let out an audible exhale. "A shame," she agreed.

As if summoned by the cosmic disturbance of their conversation, Allen glided over with a tray, each burger looking like its own little planet adorned with an olive on a toothpick flagpole. The burger buns were dyed green with food coloring, and the whole presentation was so over the top it was borderline unappetizing.

"Compliments of the cosmos," Allen said, setting down the dishes with a flourish.

"Thanks, Allen," Ethan chimed in, looking alarmed as he took in the other-worldly burger. "How's it been, taking over the diner?"

Allen sighed, the weight of the universe seemingly on his shoulders. "It's been great, in a way, but there's this black hole where Jamal used to be. I miss him."

"What were your plans before all this?" Annie asked, her voice softening.

"Engineering," Allen replied, a far-off look in his eye as if envisioning bridges on distant worlds. "But the tech sector is dead right now. So keeping a dream alive here feels right."

"Admirable," Annie nodded, respect coloring her usually stoic face.

"Excuse me, the grill's calling." Allen gave a half-hearted salute before disappearing into the kitchen's nebula of steam.

Giselle stared at her untouched burger, the chasm of what she knew—and what she couldn't say—widening. The clink of cutlery against ceramic punctuated the silence that had settled over the booth.

"Those open desert up North," Annie began, her gaze as sharp as the knife she used to slice through her space burger. "Ever been? About an hour above town, I mean. The map says there's nothing, but—"

Giselle shook her head, a frown etching lines into her brow. "A couple of times. What's this got to do with Jamal?"

"Case related," Annie replied succinctly, dabbing her lips with a napkin imprinted with little green men.

"When I was kid everyone used to drive into the desert to drink and do stupid things," Giselle said, remembering back to late nights spent under the stars. "We'd light off fireworks. Dance. Dare each other to go into the mines."

"Mines?" Annie asked, her tone hopeful.

"Yeah," Giselle shrugged. "There's a network of old mines

out there. They're abandoned. Probably hazardous. We'd play around them as kids but otherwise I never go that way. Actually… got called out there recently when some drunk tourists dared their friend to go down 'em and thought he got stuck. But the idiot had found his way out by the time I arrived." Giselle scanned the detectives up and down, then smiled. "Hope of the two of you don't make me head out that way again. If you decide to go mine-diving, at least use the buddy system.

"Noted," Ethan agreed.

"That's helpful, thank you," Annie said. "And onto our last lead… have you seen a black SUV around town recently? With tinted windows?" Annie prodded, her eyes flicking up to meet Giselle's.

"Black van?" Giselle leaned back, arms crossed. "I did, actually. Funny you should mention it…"

Annie and Ethan exchanged a glance. Maybe Harlan wasn't such a bad lead after all.

"I saw the black van about a week ago. It blew through here like it was chasing something. Or maybe running from something. I turned on my sirens and pulled onto the road to follow. That didn't stop it though."

"Details, Sheriff," Ethan urged, his voice a low rumble. He could sense that Giselle wanted to leave the subject alone.

"I was getting into my cruiser, coffee in hand. Small town woes took precedence." Giselle shrugged, her uniform slightly crumpled from the day's wear. "I could have chased it down, but at the speed it was going? You do 120 mph on roads like these and you might just lose a wheel and flip the damn car. I didn't see the point in chasing it when it's probably just another—"

"Tourist?" Annie quipped, a rare ghost of a smile twitching at her lips. "Seems like you have a lot of interesting beings come to town and the most dangerous ones are heading home from Las Vegas."

"Exactly," Giselle agreed, her mouth twitching in response. "Alien abductions are one thing; public intoxication is another beast entirely."

"I can't blame you," Ethan agreed, laughing. "I've seen some stupid things at the FBI. I always hope if I get taken out it's by a sniper rifle wielded by a cyberterrorist, and not some idiot college student tossing molotov cocktails at my cruiser."

"Exactly," Giselle grinned. "Let me go with dignity." She sighed, shaking her head. "That's why I didn't go after the black SUV. I just thought… it's heading out of town anyway. Let Vegas get 'em."

The meal was finished and the burgers— however strange they looked— were eaten without a crumb left behind. Giselle was relieved that the conversation turned to generic law enforcement. It seemed as if the detectives recognized her as one of their own. That was good. She wanted only to fly under the radar.

Annie's fork clattered to her plate, the sound sharp in the quiet diner. She pushed her plate away and reached across the table to shake Giselle's hand. "Thank you for everything. We'll be in touch, Giselle," she said, sliding out of the booth with an efficiency that spoke of a woman who wasted no time.

"Thanks for recommending the burger," Ethan added, his voice echoing Annie's urgency. "It was… weird," he shrugged.

They stood, and Giselle expected them to head for the front doors. But, instead, Ethan made a whistling sound toward the kitchen. Allen popped up from behind the grill, a question in his eyes.

"Hey, Allen," Ethan nodded. "You mind if we get a look at Jamal's office?"

Allen blanched, but then relaxed, acting as if this request was one that was made all the time.

"Sure," Allen nodded, holding a spatula in one hand. "It's back through that hall. Unlocked. Go for it."

Without another word, Annie and Ethan disappeared into the hallway that led to Jamal's office.

Giselle watched them leave, the last bite of her space burger sitting heavy in her stomach. Alone in the booth, surrounded by neon green and silver stars, she let out a breath she didn't know she'd been holding. She glanced back at the grill, where Allen avoided meeting her eyes, his focus on the greasy meat grilling in front of him.

"Out of the frying pan and into a mess," Giselle muttered to herself, eyeing the empty plates. The metaphor wasn't lost on her; half-eaten burgers, scattered fries – her life felt just as disorganized.

She reached for her coffee, the black liquid cold now. "You have all the power," Allen's words echoed in her head, but power felt like a joke when all she had were more questions than answers.

With one last look at the booth, Giselle grabbed her hat and strode out of Alien Eats, eager to get back to the RV park, where she could pretend she felt safe— at least, for a little while.

CHAPTER THIRTEEN

JAMAL'S OFFICE WAS A MESS.

Annie nudged the door open with her shoulder, her eyes sweeping over the chaos. It was a stark contrast to the kitschy UFO-themed diner outside. No neon greens or silvery greys here. Instead, earth tones dominated—the rich brown of polished wood, the deep green of lush plant leaves, and the muted gold of aged photographs. There was a grandeur here that was begging to be unleashed, but it was buried under cardboard boxes and piles of paper.

"Wow, no floating aliens," Ethan quipped as he stepped in beside her, his gaze following hers.

"Ground control to Major Tom," she responded dryly, scanning the room for those details that often spoke louder than words.

The office exuded a sense of calm professionalism, an unexpected discovery. A hefty desk anchored the space. Bookshelves lined one wall, filled not with science fiction but with business books, their spines worn from use. Their presence told Annie that Jamal's success was not an accident.

"Check this out," Ethan said, pointing to a black-and-white photo framed on the wall. It depicted a younger Jamal, grinning wide in a fry cook's outfit, like it was the best day of his life.

"From spatulas to spaceships," Annie mused, her voice laced with a hint of amusement.

"Quite the journey." Ethan's eyes moved to another photograph, this one in color, showing Jamal cutting a red ribbon in front of Alien Eats. The whole town of Rachel seemed to be there, cheering. "He had the town's heart."

"Looks like it." Annie's eyes narrowed slightly, processing the scene frozen in time. Community—something that often held more clues than a locked safe. What she'd learned about Jamal so far told her the man had no enemies. Which meant the crime was likely one of opportunity or necessity rather than revenge.

"Hey, is that a bonsai garden?" Ethan gestured toward a small collection of miniature trees by the window, their canopies meticulously trimmed.

"Seems so," Annie replied, walking over to examine the tiny forest. "Takes patience and precision to care for these. I think he would have been better served by cleaning out these boxes." She motioned at the boxes of paperwork strewn across the floor.

"Let's see what secrets his files hold before we start handing out gardening awards."

"Right behind you," Ethan said with a teasing grin as they turned their attention back to the task at hand.

Annie bent down to the first box, its lid sitting akimbo. She ripped off the lid, revealing an accordion file within, its tabs labeled with meticulous care. "*Diner Receipts*" caught her eye, and she tugged at the bulging section, spilling its contents across Jamal's desk.

"Look at this," she said, thumbing through the stack of receipts, her eyebrows climbing higher with each slip she examined. "Jamal's little eatery was raking it in."

"Who knew alien burgers could be so lucrative?"

"Jamal did," Annie thought aloud. She glanced again at the business books in shelves against the wall. "He researched. This was a man who knew what he was doing. He understood supply and demand. Rachel doesn't have any other diners. He picked a spot close to Vegas that might appeal to weary tourists, and created a destination that was worth stopping for. Smart."

Ethan leaned over her shoulder, his gaze scanning the numbers. "Tourist trap plus kitsch equals cash flow. The equation works."

"He probably makes more from this little diner than some clubs in Las Vegas," Annie said.

"Speaking of Vegas..." Ethan rifled through another part of the file, his hand emerging with glossy brochures adorned with images of flying saucers and grinning aliens. "Looks like Jamal didn't just count on roadside attraction charm."

"Let me see those." Annie snatched the brochures, flipping them open to reveal bold letters promising an *Earth-shattering dining experience.* "These advertisements must've cost a pretty penny."

"Good advertising isn't cheap, but it sure pays off." Ethan pointed to a picture of Jamal posing with tourists, all thumbs up and toothy smiles. "He had a knack for reeling them in."

"Space oddity or not, you can't deny the man had flair." Annie grinned, tossing a brochure back onto the desk. "I bet he sold more 'Galactic Shakes' than the casino sells dreams."

"High stakes and milkshakes." Ethan chuckled, shaking his head. "Only in Nevada."

"Or maybe it was the promise of alien encounters with every side of fries." Annie's laughter joined Ethan's, echoing in the stark room that once belonged to a man who had turned desert dust into dollars.

"Guess we know why he could afford such a well-manicured bonsai garden now," she quipped, closing the accordion file with a snap.

Annie's fingers brushed over the smooth surface of the desk, probing its secrets. The top drawer protested with a creak, revealing a disarray of pens, notepads, and one incongruously placed document. She plucked it from the chaos, her eyes narrowing at the header: Last Will and Testament.

"Strange," she murmured, unfolding the papers with care.

"Find something?" Ethan leaned in, his voice low, as if the walls held ears eager for gossip.

"That might be an understatement." Annie flipped through the will, each word sinking into her consciousness like stones in a pond. "Look around. Boxes of files everywhere and yet Jamal just casually leaves his Last Will and Testament in a drawer where it's easily found after he dies?"

"Too convenient," Ethan agreed.

"Way too convenient," Annie nodded, skimming the details of the document.

"What's it say?"

"Everything you'd expect," Annie shrugged. "Some donations to local charities. An investment in the local school. Jamal left the diner in Allen's care, which makes sense, considering he's the only other employee. The will itself isn't strange. Just the way it was laying here."

Annie placed the document on the desk and returned to the boxes laying on the floor, flipping lids off one by one. The first box held tax documents. The second, a collection of forks and knives. The third was another filing system, and Annie grinned when she noticed a particular tab.

"Come here," she motioned to Ethan, who joined her. Annie gestured to the accordion file, where neatly labeled tabs stood sentinel over their contents—all but one. It gaped open, empty, the label 'Will' taunting in its absence.

"This is where the will should be. Why would Jamal take it out and lay it in his desk before his murder?"

"You don't think he moved it himself," Ethan concluded, thumbing through the remaining documents.

"It doesn't match his personality profile. Jamal kept everything in boxes. Why leave such a crucial document out in the open?"

"Poor filing?"

"No," Annie's mind raced. "Intentional guidance."

"Welcome to Rachel, Nevada," Ethan said, "where even the paperwork is out of this world."

The knock at the door was sharp, almost impatient. Annie lifted an eyebrow as she caught Ethan's glance. They both turned toward the sound, their previous conversation about the will and Harlan's theories momentarily suspended.

"Shakes?" Allen's voice came through the door. "Didn't want to interrupt but I've got two milkshakes here, on the house."

"Timing," Annie muttered under her breath, before calling out, "Just a minute!"

Ethan slid the lid back on the accordion file back, an eye still on the will tucked under Annie's arm. Annie placed the document into her bag as Ethan opened the door to reveal Allen, his hands occupied with two towering milkshakes, their whipped cream peaks threatening to topple over.

"Chocolate and vanilla," Allen announced, like a waiter presenting a gourmet meal instead of milkshake diplomacy. "It's what Jamal would have done. Just a thank you, for— you know— the fact you're bringing him justice." Allen's eyes seemed to water, and he looked down, embarrassed.

"Thoughtful."

"Compliments of Alien Eats," Allen added with a smile that didn't quite reach his eyes.

"Best shakes this side of the galaxy," Allen said, finally easing into a full grin. "Don't be strangers, now."

"Wouldn't dream of it," Annie replied, sidestepping past him. The cold from the milkshake seeped through the cup and into her fingers.

"Thanks for the... hospitality," Ethan said, following

Annie's lead. His usual warmth replaced with the cool professionalism of an agent on a mission.

They took the milkshakes with them as they departed, Annie thinking the entire time about the document in her purse, and what it meant for their case.

CHAPTER FOURTEEN

FRANKIE

FRANKIE SHUFFLED papers on his desk, a nervous tick belied by the quiver in his fingers. The RV office felt more cramped than usual, even though he had cleaned it twice just this afternoon. The distinct smell of old coffee and sweat—which Frankie had never been able to get out of the carpets when he bought the RV second-hand— clung to the air.

Overhead, fluorescent lights flickered, casting an unflattering glow on everything in the room, and reminding Frankie he had failed to get the bulb fixed. Across from him, Annie's sharp gaze cut through the clutter, while Ethan's imposing frame seemed to absorb the space.

"Jamal, and the diner," Annie began, her voice razor-sharp, "We'd love to know what you thought about him, as a person, and about his business."

"Ah, Jamal," Frankie said, straightening his tie as if he were interviewing for a job. "Those green hamburger buns were something else. I thought he was a good business owner, just like me."

"Harlan says he saw a UFO the night before he died," Annie added. "Did you know about that? You didn't mention it when we arrived…"

Frankie threw his hands in the air. "Harlan says a lot of crazy stuff. I've learned to tune most of it out."

Ethan leaned forward, casting a long shadow over Frankie's collection of novelty pens. "And Bianca's cameras? They're everywhere. What's your take? Could she be involved?"

"Involved?" Frankie snorted. "She's just cashing in on the paranoia. She takes advantage of the UFO hype just like the rest of us. The renewed interest in aliens was the best thing that ever happened to the town of Rachel. And Bianca couldn't hurt a fly. She's just a regular old opportunist. In fact, I can't think of one person who had it out for Jamal. Not one. The man was a Saint. Loved around these parts. Just like me," Fankie puffed out his chest. "People around here like aspirational business owners. Jamal and I are both kind of a big deal."

"I can see that," Annie nodded at him, encouraging. "That's why we wanted to talk to you again. Because you're such an important member of the community. We thought you might know…"

"Yes?"

"About the black van that's been driving around. Harlan mentioned it to us."

"Harlan's a conspiracy theorist."

"Problem is…" Annie said. "Harlan's not the only one who's seen it."

Frankie's fingers drummed a staccato rhythm on the faux-wood desk, the hollow sound barely audible over the hum of the air conditioner wheezing its last breaths. He eyed Annie and Ethan, their faces expectant, waiting for him to dispel or confirm the town's latest ghost story.

"Black van?" he scoffed, shaking his head as his bony shoulders lifted in a shrug. "It belongs in the same category as aliens and government spies." A playful smirk played at the corners of his mouth. "I focus on what's real, which is money and RVs."

"Are deserted mines more your speed, then?" Annie queried, her gaze sharp. "Jamal's case isn't the only one we're working on. We came out here for a different case. One that's personal. And I think it might involve the desert an hour North of town. Giselle told us the only thing out there is some old mines. Know anything about them?"

"Sure thing." Frankie leaned forward, the chair groaning under the sudden shift. He pulled open a drawer, rummaging through tourist brochures and expired coupons until his hand emerged clutching a colorful pamphlet. *The Desert's Wonders*, it proclaimed in bold letters above a picture of a rugged landscape.

"Check this out," he unfolded the brochure with a flourish, pointing to a craggy rock formation that looked like tetris played with boulders. "I give these pamphlets to tourists who want to do a desert drive. The mines are burrowed right underneath that rock formation there. I used to stop by as a kid..."

"Did you... *make* this?" Annie said, appearing impressed.

"I did," Frankie nodded, his face flushing with pride. "I'm pretty good with digital photo editing. I made these pamphlets for guests, along with all our ads. I even made some flyers for Jamal to advertise the diner out in Vegas."

"We saw them!" Annie exclaimed. "In his office. Those were beautiful. We assumed he paid a designer."

"Nope," Frankie pumped out his chest. "All me. I helped with all the advertising. You know, one business owner to another."

Frankie opened up the pamphlet, laying it flat so Annie and Ethan could see the images of the desert. There was a picture of the entrance to the mines, as well as an odd rock formation and a stunning sunset. "Now, I know the best spots in the desert because I used to hang out there as a kid."

"Old playground?" Ethan asked, eyes flickering with interest.

"Yep," Frankie replied, nostalgia softening his voice. "We'd pretend we were treasure hunters... or on the run from bandits. My friends and I grew up playing near those mines. I know 'em like the back of my hand. Not the brightest idea, but there isn't a lot to do out here for a kid."

"They span quite the distance," Annie pressed, all business again. "What's the best way to access them?"

"North side's easiest." Frankie traced a route with his forefinger, ending on a cartoonish depiction of a miner's cart. "There's an entrance over here. You can head down until the light disappears, and then open up the silver door that says *Do Not Enter*. Head further down and you can see the stalactite formations, but stop when you hit the mine carts. Any further and you're asking for trouble."

"What kind of trouble?" Ethan asked.

Frankie shrugged. "Natural gas. Cave-ins. All kinds of things." Frankie paused. "I should add that I usually warn tourists just to look at the outside, take some photos. You're not supposed to go inside."

"Got it." Annie nodded, her mind clearly already mapping their nocturnal expedition.

"Best years of my life," Frankie said, though his smile didn't quite reach his eyes. "Playing cowboys and miners, dreaming of striking gold."

"You must have had a great childhood in Rachel. And the RV park?" Annie gestured towards a faded photograph pinned to the corkboard—a younger Frankie with a plump, smiling woman who could only be his grandmother.

"Grandma's pride and joy," he said with genuine affection, tilting his head toward the photo. A smile crossed his face and Frankie seemed to light up. Then, as if on cue, his hand dipped back into the desk, emerging with a creased document that he pulled from a folder. He slid the land deed across to them, the motion too smooth— rehearsed. Annie couldn't help but think Frankie had been waiting for this moment. "You can see the deed, right here. It's a real important symbol of what's been in my family for generations."

"Family heirloom, huh?" Ethan quipped, leaning in to scrutinize the paper.

"Something like that," Frankie answered, the words tasting of old secrets and dusty lies.

Annie's eyes lingered on the deed, but Frankie could see her gears turning, piecing together a puzzle only she could see. "That is… some kind of paper," Annie smiled at him as if he were a student failing a test. She ran her hand over the gold stamp that marked its edge, and for the first time, Frankie realized that delivering the document from his printer meant the seal wasn't embossed. It sat flat against the page, lifeless. "What I mean to say," Annie continued, "Is that it's very well *designed.*"

Frankie shivered, and his eyes locked onto Annie's. There was a silent understanding between them, and it was one that made Frankie's heart race. For a moment, the RV felt less like an office and more like a stage, with Frankie playing his part to an audience of two who were always one step ahead.

"I'm a good business owner," Frankie said weakly, thinking about his Grandma and what she'd left him. "I always have my paperwork ready."

"Thanks for the history lesson," Annie said, standing up in a way that caused her shoes to click on the worn linoleum floor.

"Anytime," Frankie echoed, his relief a quiet shadow passing behind his grin. He took back the deed and returned it to its place inside the folder, then pushed the tourist pamphlet toward them. "For visiting the mines, nighttime is best," he said. "Less heat, more... ambiance. And if you're doing to what I told you *not* to do and go inside, less prying eyes to phone it in."

"Thanks, Frankie," Annie said

"Watch out for bats," he added, a half-hearted attempt at levity as they turned towards the door.

"Love bats," Ethan threw over his shoulder, a smirk playing on his lips.

"Good luck," Frankie called after them, but the RV door had already clicked shut, sealing off his words in the empty space.

He slumped back into his chair, the faux leather squeaking under his weight. A bead of sweat traced its way down his neck as he replayed their conversation, searching for missteps. *Was I convincing enough?* he thought to himself.

"Should've taken up acting," he muttered to the silence, his chuckle hollow. He eyed the file with the land deed still lying on the desk, the forgery now glaringly obvious in the harsh light of his solitude. "Damn it," he hissed, snatching the paper and shoving it back into its hiding spot. It was done. His part was played.

Annie's piercing eyes and Ethan's squared jaw haunted the edges of his vision. They were good people, just doing their job, wrapped up in the chaos he'd helped create.

Frankie stood, pacing the tiny confines of his office-turned-prison. Tonight, the mines would either be their salvation or his downfall. And Frankie? He had one more role to play.

He knew what he had to do. He just wished things could have gone differently— the detectives seemed like nice people.

CHAPTER FIFTEEN

IT WAS dark when Annie and Ethan loaded the pickup truck with supplies, and nighttime in the desert hit differently. The sound of crickets singing echoed across the blackened blanket of sand, the scent of the day still clinging to the air. Ethan groaned as he dropped a plastic quart of water into the bed of the truck.

"Feels like we're going to the moon and not an hour North," Ethan said, shaking his head.

"Just in case something goes wrong," Annie shrugged, looking at the food supplies and water they'd loaded into white pickup. "Plan for the best, prepare for the worst." Annie didn't want to admit it, but she'd been on edge since they'd arrived in the town of Rachel, and extra supplies was her way of coping with the feeling. Ethan seemed to know as much, because he hadn't complained about the trip to the general store, or the work of loading it all into the truck. "Just in case the car breaks down, or someone intercepts us—" Annie said, feeling the need to explain without voicing her every fear aloud.

"You think The Collective is already out here?" Ethan asked, referencing the shadow organization they'd sworn to destroy. "I don't see how they could know about Russel's compound before us—"

"I think they're here," Annie nodded. "But not in a way that's dangerous for us."

"Hudson, I'm 'gonan need you to stop talking in riddles one day," Ethan laughed.

"That day is not today," Annie said, slamming the truck's back hatch shut.

"Are you ready?" Ethan asked, leaning against the driver's side. He looked good like this, and it wasn't lost on Annie. The desert had done right by Ethan— a fact that Annie noticed with surprise. Usually, Ethan shrunk a little in remote locations. He did better in cities, where there was always life to lived and activities to be shared. But the desert had expanded him. He looked broader somehow, as if he were growing into himself.

"Ready," Annie agreed, hopping into the passenger seat. She settled in, reaching into her bag and unfolding two paper documents. One was the map drawn by Fleur. The other was the tourist pamphlet from Frankie. Annie pointed at the pamphlet, motioning to how it overlayed with Fleur's draw-ing. "Same quadrant," Annie said. "The mines line up. I don't *know* that Russel's compound is there, but there's not much else out in this section of the desert. It's a hunch, but a good one."

"If it's not the mines, it's something else," Ethan said out loud, more for himself than for Annie. "A rock formation. Or a cave. Whatever it is, we'll find it."

The van's tires squealed as they went into motion, leaving Rachel behind and starting the long drive down a road that hardly looked like a road at all. It was a carved slice of path in the desert sand, taking them into the distance where there were no lights— only stretches of emptiness.

As they drove north into the inky desert night, Ethan drummed his fingers on the steering wheel, lost in thought.

The truck's headlights cut through the darkness, illuminating the narrow ribbon of highway stretching endlessly ahead.

"Do you think they're really out there?" Ethan asked suddenly, glancing over at Annie with a teasing look. "Aliens, I mean."

Annie looked up from the maps, surprised by the question. She studied Ethan's profile, his chiseled features cast in stark relief by the dashboard lights. "Jamal's story got to you, huh?" She smiled at him. "Do *you* think he was killed by aliens? Or a government cover up related to aliens?"

"Nope," Ethan said, shaking his head. "I don't think aliens are real because I don't believe in anything I can't see."

Annie sat up, surprised by this new information. She realized then that— as long as they'd known each other— she had never thought to ask Ethan what he believed in, if anything. "So, you're an atheist?" she asked.

"I'm not anything," Ethan answered. He looked out at the empty night, seeing nothing there. "I deal with what's in front of me and that's it. But if you're asking whether I think aliens visit the Earth— no, I don't. People like to imagine beyond what they can see because they're wishing for more than they've got."

"Huh," Annie answered in that quiet way of hers. Ethan caught the tone.

"You don't agree?"

"I think the most *interesting* things are the things we can't see," Annie answered.

"But you always say suspicions aren't facts—"

"Until they lead to one," Annie said. "But that a suspicion can lead to a fact at all is quite interesting, don't you think? Where does that come from? From places unknown."

"Annie Hudson," Ethan let out a low whistle. "You're full of surprises."

"I'm afraid this case will be as well… especially for you," Annie said to him, her voice a low whisper. Then, she slapped her hands on her lap as if she'd just realized something wonderful. "Alright, so you don't believe in aliens. You only believe in what you can see. How then, does a man like you ever *hope*? Hope for better days? Hope for promises made?"

"Simple," Ethan laughed. "I don't hope. I let what happens— happen. And if it's to my liking, I feel very thankful for that. And when it's not, I let it go and don't think about it."

"Hmm," Annie said, thinking back to their childhood and remembering what they'd lost. "I guess— in your case— hope could be a trap, couldn't it? My brother— they found his body— but for you—"

"Yeah," Ethan agreed. "That was rough. That they never found Megan's body." Annie jolted at hearing Ethan use his sister's name. It was a rare occurrence. Usually, he referenced Megan as "his sister" as if he was trying to keep some distance. The use of her name drove home that she had been a person— a person who was no longer with them. "I saw the pain hoping caused my Mother," Ethan continued. "She hoped for years, and nothing ever came of it. Would've been kinder if there'd been no room to hope. So, I decided a long time ago to live in the now. I told myself I wasn't 'gonna believe in what I can't see. My sister is gone— just like your brother— and I have to focus on destroying the person who broke my family. On bringing justice into the world any chance I get in honor of her memory."

Annie nodded, leaning back in the passenger seating and watching a blur of charcoal desert zip by.

"What're you thinking about, Hudson?" Ethan asked.

"I was just wondering…" Annie said, dragging a finger over the fogging glass of the window, a circle appearing under her touch. "What non-believers will do when a UFO lands right in front of them?"

"Shit themselves, probably," Ethan laughed. He glanced at Annie, noting the seriousness in her expression. "You really *do* believe in aliens, don't you?" Ethan exclaimed, shocked to find that the most reasonable person he'd ever known believed in something so— childish.

"I do," Annie nodded. "And one day, you will too."

Ethan shook his head, his features darkening as he turned back to the endless stretch of road in front of him that needed tending to. "I will, huh?"

"You will," Annie said. "When a spaceship lands right in front of you. I only hope you can survive the shock." There was a dark edge of concern to Annie's voice that made Ethan wonder— *what did she know?* Annie was always two steps ahead of him, but now, it seemed as if she were walking a path he couldn't follow. A shiver ran down Ethan's spine, but he shook it away. He wanted to ask more— to probe Annie's brilliant mind for answers. But instead, he kept his hands on the wheel, watching as the desert unfolded. For some people, it might be filled with mysteries. But for Ethan, the desert was a stretch of empty dirt— meaningless and lacking.

And he liked it that way.

The thought that such a thing could ever change made him feel adrift.

He glanced back at Annie, who sat silently in the passenger seat, her brilliant mind whirring over something that he could feel— but couldn't understand.

CHAPTER SIXTEEN

GISELLE

THE SIZZLE of onions and peppers hit the hot skillet, a sharp hiss filling the cramped kitchen of Giselle's RV as she stirred the pot. The aroma of cumin and garlic mingled with the desert night creeping in through the half-open window. Maria— Giselle's mother, a brusque woman in her eighties— was at the stove, her fingers nimble despite her years. Deftly rolled tortillas landed on the worn Formica countertop.

"Met with the detectives today," Giselle said, dumping a can of beans into the mix. "They're chasing their tails now, looking elsewhere."

Maria clucked her tongue, pressing a tortilla flat with the palm of her hand. "*Mija,* just tell them everything. It would be better—"

"You know why I can't." Giselle slashed the air with her spatula.

Maria waved a hand in the air as if the issue— which they'd discussed each day since Jamal's passing— was unimportant. "Blackmail," Maria shook her head. "The strategy of a coward. You are better than that. Ignore the threat and do what you know is right."

"*No puedo,*" Giselle shook her head. "I can't. Not when it involves you."

Maria took a sip from the pot, tasting the broth of what was within. "So the blackmailer calls ICE on me. *¿Así que lo que?* That's life. At least I'll know you've done what's right—"

"You won't feel the same when you're carted off—"

"*¡Dios Mio!*" Maria exclaimed, but then her face set, stubborn and unyielding. "You think I'm scared? I crossed the Rio Grande; I can handle an empty-headed bully."

"That's great for you but not for me. I can't allow it to happen." Giselle scooped out some of the bean mixture onto a plate, the contents spitting like a cornered cat. "All of this is unfair. Jamal's murder. The system. The fact we're kept so vulnerable. If life's unfair to me, I'll hit back at life."

"No," Maria said, flipping another tortilla with a flick of her wrist, "*El que con lobos anda, a aullar se enseñat.* If you act like those who hurt you, you become what you hate!" Maria stopped, placing a hand on her daughter's cheek. "Where's the girl I raised? The one who believed in justice? That's the girl who became a Sheriff! She would tell the truth!"

"Even when the truth could cost you everything?" Giselle countered, her hand hovering over the handle of the sizzling pan, the heat radiating onto her already flushed face.

"Jamal was a friend," Maria said, dropping the lettuce as if releasing a burden. "If you know something about his death, you bring justice. You took an oath. *Es tu deber.*"

Giselle turned away, focusing on the clink of cutlery, the scrape of spatula on skillet. Yet her mind raced, thoughts slicing through the clutter. She had lied to the detectives. She had broken her oath. But— as she watched her elderly mother laying plates on the table— she still felt she'd had no other choice. She'd learned in her years as Sheriff that the law wasn't always good, and what was good wasn't always legal.

Jamal would have wanted Giselle to protect the people

who mattered most to her. And Giselle intended to do just that— no matter the cost.

"I can't tell them Mama," Giselle said, shaking her head. Tears formed in her eyes, but she wouldn't let them fall. "They're good detectives. They'll just have to figure it out on their own."

CHAPTER SEVENTEEN

BIANCA

THE NIGHT AIR WAS CRISP, and the stars above Rachel, Nevada, winked at Bianca as if they were in on the joke. She smirked, adjusting the fishing wire that tethered her makeshift silver disks to the barren branches of a Joshua tree. With her camera perched on a tripod, she hit record, the red light blinking like a beacon of conspiracy.

"Prepare for lift-off, Earthlings," she whispered with a chuckle, gently shaking the wire to set the 'UFOs' into an otherworldly dance.

"Watch out, Area 51, you've got competition." Her voice was a mix of mischief and mock gravity as she narrated her own footage. The silver disks wobbled unconvincingly against the ink-black sky, their movements more seasick than extraterrestrial.

"Oscar-worthy special effects," Bianca mused aloud, scanning her viewfinder for the best angle. "Eat your heart out, Spielberg." She knew she would edit the footage later and— through a mix of practical effects and editing magic— create something mind-blowing, albeit— fake.

Headlights pierced the darkness, and a white pick-up truck roared past, dust billowing in its wake. Bianca squinted, catching sight of the unmistakable profiles of Annie and Ethan inside, their expressions tight with purpose. "Detectives Annie Hudson and Agent Ethan Beckett, off to save the world again," she said under her breath, offering a mock salute.

As the truck's tail lights vanished over the horizon, another vehicle crept into view. Bianca froze. She crouched low, making sure the vehicle couldn't see her.

A black SUV glided by, ghostlike. The way it moved was strange— noiseless, creeping just below the speed limit. Its headlights were off even in the black of night. It moved with predatory smoothness, edging along the road, following the detectives' trail like a shadow clinging to the heels of its prey.

"Sketchy," Bianca quipped, though a thread of unease wound through her. She grabbed her camera and peered through the lens, zooming in on the SUV's retreating form. She recorded the van as it loomed into the distance.

The laugh that bubbled up felt forced, the humor now tinged with the cold prickling of suspicion. She kept filming, half-expecting men in black suits to pop out and demand her memory on a platter.

With a last glance at the ominous SUV, Bianca's instincts kicked into overdrive. She dashed to her DIY set-up, yanking fake silver disks from the sky and coiling fishing wire with deft fingers. Her camera—a trusty sidekick in her quest for extraterrestrial fame—was snapped shut and stuffed into its padded bag. The cool desert air held a charge tonight, one that whispered of more than just pretend alien invasions.

They don't need your help, Bianca thought to herself. The Detectives were grown people. Still, Bianca considered what she'd done, and everything she'd lied about. She remembered the harddrive hiding in the back of her van, which hid the biggest lie she'd ever told. Bigger, even, than her fraudulent videos.

I have to do the right thing.

"Time to jet," she muttered, slinging the bag over her shoulder. Gravel crunched underfoot as she sprinted to her pink van. She chucked the equipment haphazardly into the back, slammed the door, and revved the engine to life. Tires spat out pebbles as she peeled away, leaving behind only dust and the echo of her departure.

Minutes later, Bianca skidded into the RV park, the car's headlights cutting swathes through the darkness. She parked with a jerk, barely waiting for the engine to die before jumping out. Her pink hair caught the moonlight, turning it into a beacon as she navigated between the hulking shadows of RVs.

"Harlan! Open up!" she rapped on his door, urgency thrumming in her veins like a bassline. "It's Bianca—"

The door creaked open, revealing Harlan's bushy beard and skeptical gaze. "What's got you more rattled ?"

"I believe you," she said breathlessly. "I saw it, Harlan. The black SUV. It was creeping on Annie and Ethan. They were heading North— I don't know why—"

"We have to help them," Bianca said, her stomach churning. "I've done a lotta wrong things in my life but if the SUV is really dangerous like you said—"

"We need one more person," Harlan nodded, grabbing his coat and slamming the door behind him. He descended down the RV steps, Bianca bobbing in his wake.

Harlan stopped when he reached Giselle's trailer, wrapping on the door. The Sheriff opened it, and the smell of dinner wafted into the air.

"Harlan? Bianca?" Giselle asked, surprised at the visit.

"No time," Harlan waved a hand in the air. "The black SUV is following Annie and Ethan. Bianca saw it. They're heading North."

Giselle's mind raced to catch up. "North?" She asked, wondering what on Earth would make them want to head into the desert. Then, she remembered her earlier conversation with the Detectives. "They asked me about the mines," Giselle realized out loud. "I wonder if they're chasing a lead."

"I think the lead is chasing *them*," Harlan corrected her. "They need our help. That black SUV is on their tail."

Giselle paused, considering that all her problems might go away if she just let nature take its course. If the person in the black SUV had plans, maybe it would be best to let them execute them.

Giselle glanced over her shoulder at her Mom, seated at the table, a knowing look in her eyes.

"Let's go," she said, descending down the steps.

"I'll drive," Bianca added, and with that, the trio took off into the night.

CHAPTER EIGHTEEN

THE DESERT STRETCHED OUT SO FAR— with such darkness— that Annie and Ethan almost missed the entrance to the mines. When the entrance revealed itself as a wooden structure looming off the beaten path, Ethan slammed the truck into park, gravel crunching beneath the tires. He threw the transmission into reverse, then delicately guided the truck off the road, its wheels straining against the untamed desert floor. The stark beams of the truck's headlights carved a swath through the darkness, revealing the gaping maw of the mine's entrance. There was a humming sound before Ethan turned the key over in the ignition, as if the truck knew they'd arrived at their destination and was bidding them farewell.

"Not much to look at, is it?" Ethan asked Annie. They leaned forward, peering out the windows at the entrance to the mines. Rusty tracks led into the abyss, framed by timber supports that groaned with age. Shadows clung to the jagged rocks like cobwebs. Deserted for years, the mine now served as a threshold to secrets buried deep within its belly— and it looked as if it didn't wish to be disturbed.

"Cheery place," Annie quipped, opening the passenger-side door and stepping out into the chill night air. She zipped up her jacket, her breath visible in the headlights' glare.

"Nothing says 'welcome' like rotting wooden support beams," Ethan replied, locking the truck behind him as he followed Annie into the darkness. His gaze lingered on the mine, a sentinel warning them of the danger ahead.

"Remember when our biggest worry was who borrowed whose CDs?" Annie chuckled, her eyes glinting with the reflection of their past. "Now here we are, about to solve the crime that changed our lives forever—"

"Ah yes, the great CD heist of '98." Ethan smirked, remembering the summer before his sister disappeared, in which he and Annie had tried to solve the disappearance of a collection of CDs at their local high school. If he'd known then that his own sister would become the subject of an investigation, he never would have tried to play Detective in the first place. Secretly, Ethan had always wondered if their games had somehow led to the real-life crime that changed both their trajectories forever. It was magical thinking, and he knew it wasn't true. Still, some piece of him felt guilty for playing Detective, never knowing tragedy would make him a real one.

"This is the first step in making it right," Annie said, staring into the mouth of the mine.

"It's been a thousand little steps, Hudson," Ethan answered, shaking his head. "None of them leading anywhere. And now— we're about to get lost."

"Speak for yourself, Beckett. I never get lost." Annie's voice held a playful confidence, but her mind churned, piecing together every detail they had uncovered so far.

"You just take unexpected detours."

"Exactly. All part of the plan."

They stood side by side, staring into the darkness. A moment passed, laden with the weight of what lay ahead.

"Hard to believe it's come down to this," Ethan murmured,

his thoughts drifting to his sister, whose eyes he could never forget. The pictures on the wanted poster hadn't done them justice. Ethan remembered them as they *really* were— endless pools of grey with a jagged edge around the irises. "You and me against the unknown."

"Russel's puzzles led us here," Annie added, thinking of her own brother, whose death had propelled her into this life of investigation. "If his compound is down there, we'll find it. We'll figure out how we can track down The Collective. We'll make sure they can never hurt anyone else."

"Our siblings would be proud," Ethan said, a half-smile tugging at his lips.

"Or at least entertained," Annie countered. They shared a fleeting grin, a silent acknowledgment of the bond forged between them by shared purpose and parallel losses.

"Let's solve this mystery, Hudson." Ethan's voice was firm, resolute.

"Right behind you," Annie nodded, her determination unyielding as they stepped towards the mine's entrance. Her boots crunched over rocks as she descended into the mouth of the mine, Ethan's flashlight lighting the way as it unfolded before them. Iron tracks carved a path into the darkness, and Annie imagined Russel entering the caverns in the same fashion. She wondered if he'd been afraid. At the thought of Russel, Annie reached into her jacket pocket, closing her hand around Russel's plastic access card. She knew the card was in her pocket, but found herself frequently checking for its presence as if it were a lucky penny.

"Still got the card?" Ethan asked, reading Annie's mind.

"You think I'd come this far to lose it?" Annie pretended to be offended.

The opening behind them was no longer visible as the pair pushed further into the gaping maw carved into the mountain side. The tunnel was framed by timeworn wooden beams. Stagnant air filled Annie's nostrils, laced with the tang of earth and the mustiness of disuse. With each step into the mines, shadows stretched and contorted around them—specters dancing just out of sight.

"I could get used to this," Annie observed dryly, her voice echoing slightly against the rough walls. "Not too unfriendly a place."

"Could use a heater," Ethan said as they navigated around an overturned ore cart, its rusted wheels silent witnesses to a bygone era of toil. He shivered, pulling his jacket tighter around his shoulders. "I thought deserts were supposed to be warm."

"Not at night," Annie answered. She paused, noticing shapes up ahead. Ethan stepped forward, shining his flashlight on the emerging obstacles yards away. Abandoned equipment lay scattered, skeletal remains of industry. Broken lights hung from the ceiling, their glass shattered, the filaments long since burned out. Ethan passed Annie the flashlight, reaching into his backpack to pull out his electronic tablet. He turned it on, a digital glow casting a blue light over his face. His fingers grazed over the glass as he pulled up a sketch of the mines he'd received from Milo, who had commandeered a couple of satellites to create a map of the underground fortress.

"Milo's map is good," Ethan nodded. "We need to proceed about five hundred more feet before we see the split."

"And to think, you didn't even like Milo when you first met him," Annie smiled.

Ethan tucked the tablet back into his backpack while Annie played her flashlight over a pile of splintered wood and twisted metal.

"That's because he breaks every law he can," Ethan shrugged. "But I have to admit, I don't mind when he's breaking them for *me*."

The musty air clung to their lungs as they navigated deeper, the truck's headlights a fading memory. They passed the abandoned carts, stopping when they reached a solid, metal door inconspicuously wedged between the weathered timber supports. It blocked the passageway, cutting off their progress. Annie ran a hand over its metal rivets.

"Doesn't exactly look original to the mines, does it?" she quipped, her voice echoing slightly across the cavernous space.

"Russel?" Ethan's query dangled in the stale air like a challenge.

"Who else could it be?" Annie shot back, nudging the door with her boot. It didn't budge.

Ethan joined Annie, and together they heaved against the cold steel. It groaned open in protest, and Annie jammed a sizeable rock at its base to keep it open. Together, Annie and Ethan peered into the rest of the tunnel

"If Milo is right, the split should be just a little further down," Ethan offered. "But I hope Russel didn't leave this door as a—"

"Trap?" Annie asked.

Ethan didn't answer, but instead sighed heavily, making his way into the remainder of the tunnel. His flashlight illuminated the space as they progresses deeper into the belly of the beast, stopping when— just as Milo had predicted— they landed at a fork in the road. The mine cart tracks split in two directions, both of which looked exactly the same. Left or right? The tunnels branched, offering two paths wrapped in darkness. Left bore a faint draft; right, a silence that seemed to hum.

"Well, Hudson? What's it 'gonna be?" Ethan asked. "Left or right?"

Annie paused, taking in the available information.

"Left."

"Dare I ask why?"

"It smells less like despair," Annie decided, wrinkling her nose.

"Your nose ever wrong?" Ethan asked, half-joking as he followed her lead.

"Only when I thought your cologne was a good idea," she teased, stepping over a fallen beam.

"Ouch," he said, but admiration flickered in his eyes for her unerring instinct.

The pair walked for what felt like hours in the darkness—but when Annie checked her watch, only twenty minutes had passed. Still, the tunnel unfolded before them with a mocking repetition that made time seem to stand still. The tunnel's path brought them deeper into the Earth at a sharp incline, and Annie wondered how far they could go without needing to worry about air quality. Finally, they reached it: the tunnel's end. Annie's breath quickened as she saw the dead end up ahead, hoping to find an access door.

Instead, the tunnel's end loomed like a cruel joke. A wall of earth and stone sealed their way, mocking them with its impassive finality. Annie grabbed the flashlight from Ethan, lighting up the wall as if she might have missed something. She searched the packed Earth for any sign of a door or electronic access panel. Nothing.

"Great," Annie grumbled. She hated being wrong. Luckily, such a thing happened rarely in her world.

"Your nose is off. Maybe my cologne *isn't* so bad." Ethan quipped, his voice bouncing off the close walls of their rocky dead-end alcove.

Annie shot him a glare. "We'll go back to the split and try the other direction," she said.

"Right after this," Ethan smiled at her, reaching into his bag once again and pulling out a small, rectangular sensor. He placed it against the dirt wall, hitting a button on the side that made an indicator light on the sensor's edge flash green. "Milo can use this to map the mines for us. The overhead scan isn't very detailed. He said if I left one of these babies deeper, he could get us a better image."

"I'm impressed," Annie said, meaning. She preferred old-fashioned methods of detective work, like interviewing suspects and relying on a network of details. But Ethan and Mile had outdone themselves, here.

Once the sensor was in place, Annie and Ethan reversed, walking up the incline from which they'd come.

They were halfway up the tunnel when it happened:

Ethan's boot found an unfaithful rock. It betrayed him, sending his arms pinwheeling. He caught himself, but the damage was done. There was a sound of shifting stones, jarring in the stillness—a prelude to chaos.

"Move!" Ethan's shout spiked with urgency as the tunnel threatened to erase itself from existence.

They sprinted back toward the promise of open space, lungs burning with dust and adrenaline, boots thundering in a rhythm with their pounding hearts. Behind them, the earth crumbled, collapsing with the petulance of a child tearing down a block tower. The sides of the tunnel began to fold in on themselves, old rocks that used to hold up the side walls falling with ease.

Ethan threw himself over Annie to cover her just as the echoing sound became unbearable. And then— stillness. Nothing but a cool, gentle silence. Annie and Ethan untangled themselves, looking behind them at the damage. The rocks almost fully blocked the tunnel, making a second look at the dead end impossible.

"I don't think Russel's compound could have been down that tunnel," Annie shook her head. "He came and went enough that he would have made sure to clear out hazards. It has to be the other tunnel."

"Let's hope so," Ethan answered, nodding at the pile of rocks that blocked the way back. They were out of options. Forward was their only choice. Together, they stood, making their way back toward the split. When they reached it, Annie gazed into the other tunnel, feeling something stir within her.

Russel's compound was there. Annie knew it. She was about to step into the darkness when Ethan whistled at her.

"Hudson," he said, the fear that coated his voice making Annie shiver. Ethan was rarely afraid. "You're 'gonna wanna see this."

Annie turned, looking into the main tunnel where Ethan was shining his light. There, a few hundred yards away, the metal door shone in the darkness. It was closed, sealed as if by an invisible hand. The rock Annie had slid against its silver frame was nowhere to be found.

"Maybe it's an optical illusion," Annie said, knowing that it most certainly was not an illusion.

"Should we find out?" Ethan asked, the resignation in his voice telling her that he knew what *she* knew. They ran toward the door, stopping when they reached it. Annie kicked the rock, which was now discarded off to the side.

"Seriously?! Did the rock go on break?" Annie lamented, her hands pushing against the immovable door.

"Must've joined a union," Ethan said, scanning the frame for any sign of their makeshift doorstop.

Together, they pushed hard on the metal door's frame. It didn't budge.

"Perfect." Annie exhaled, her breath visible in the flashlight's beam. "I hope those are new batteries in that flashlight. We might need it for awhile."

"New batteries, but old luck," Ethan muttered, their laughter echoing off the walls, mingling with the distant rumbles of the earth settling into its new form.

"Old luck's got nothing on us, Beckett." Annie steadied herself with resolve, the light in her eyes not solely from the flashlight. "We're writing a new fortune tonight."

Annie tried to sound encouraging, but her voice fell flat against the darkness. She thought about the supplies loaded in the back of the pick-up truck, which was parked outside the mines, out of reach. Annie had prepared for every possible danger, except for the most obvious one. She wondered if the personal nature of the case— if the pain she felt when she thought about her brother's murder— had made her lose her edge. The stale air of the mines filled her lungs, and it occurred to her that no one except Milo knew where they were headed. They were trapped in the darkness with no hope of rescue. And— unless something changed— they might die without locating Russel's compound. The silence burned Annie's ears as she allowed her brilliant mind to scan all possible options, seeking a way out— an answer to the puzzle.

But despite her best efforts, no answer came.

"Hudson?" Ethan asked.

"I'm working on it," Annie answered.

Ethan took in her expression, realizing it was one he had never seen before. It was rare Annie found herself stumped. Ethan set down the flashlight and moved back to the door, his fingers curving around the metal handle. He pushed with all his weight, but the door didn't budge.

They were trapped. That was clear. But Ethan continued to rage against the door, refusing to give up— without a fight.

CHAPTER NINETEEN

FRANKIE

OUTSIDE THE MINES, the crickets were singing, and the evening was an ordinary one. The little insects chirped, unaware two people were trapped in the Earth below.

Frankie's knuckles whitened as he gripped the steering wheel, his gaze fixed on the mouth of the mines like a hawk eyeing prey. He had done something awful. Something he *should* be held accountable for. But Frankie knew life was unfair, and bad people were rarely held to account. He hoped this rule would work in his favor, at least for tonight.

You should let them out, Frankie thought, his heart pounding. *Just go down there and open up the door so they can get out. Pretend it was an accident. Tell them it wasn't you.*

Frankie shivered, fighting his own desire to leap from his car and do the right thing. He knew his Grandmother would be disappointed in him. She was a liar, but not a murderer. Frankie had taken the con too far, and now, he had become someone he didn't recognize. If only the Detectives had been so insistent about poking around.

Frankie debated, looking at his reflection in the rearview mirror. He fiddled with the radio, turning down the volume as a sad country song came on. He considered driving away, but something about leaving seemed so *final.*

Surely, when the Sheriff ultimately found the bodies, she would think the Detectives getting stuck in the mine was an accident. There were no cameras out here. No witnesses. Frankie knew if he left now, nobody would be the wiser. But still, he'd have to live with the knowledge of what he'd done forever.

Frankie was about to get out of the car when he heard an engine purring in the distance, growing louder until headlights sliced through the dusk and a vehicle rolled to a stop near the mine's mine entrance. Frankie's headlights were off and he was far enough away to avoid discovery, but still— he slumped down in his seat to avoid being seen. He peeked over the steering wheel at the intruder, who arrived in a bright, pink RV that he knew well.

Bianca, Frankie thought, surprised. The doors to the RV creaked open and out popped Bianca, her pink hair glowing like a neon sign against the drab desert backdrop. Harlan followed her, beard first, looking like some kind of hipster Moses about to part a sea of dirt. Giselle was next in line, wearing pajamas instead of her usual Sheriff's uniform.

Bianca, Harlan… and Giselle? Working together?

"Strange," Frankie muttered under his breath, an eyebrow arching in amusement. He hadn't pegged Bianca and Harlan for heroes Then again, with those two, anything that screamed conspiracy or extraterrestrial was akin to catnip. The presence of Giselle meant the law was now involved. Frankie would be lucky if got away unseen.

Bianca pulled out a DSLR camera, clipping a circular light to its surface. She flipped the screen around and appeared to be recording herself. She tried to point it at Harlan, but he pushed it away. Giselle led the group and, together, they shuffled into the dark maw of the mines, their silhouettes swallowed by shadows.

Frankie's fingers drummed on the steering wheel, a staccato beat against the silence. It seemed he didn't need to make any decisions, now. Bianca and Harlan would find the Detectives. They'd taken care of the problem for him. There was nothing left to do but go home, and pray for mercy.

His heart-pounding, Frankie threw his car into gear, tires spinning in the dirt as he made his way back to the main road. Then, he saw it:

A black SUV parked in the desert dust.

It was far enough away from the mines that it blended in with the horizon, but close enough that the person within could see everything. The vehicle was difficult to make out against the dark blanket of night, but when a light clicked on in one of the shaded windows, the SUV was illuminated, if only briefly. The car was parked in such a way that the mines were fully visible from within.

Frankie slammed on his breaks, staring at the SUV.

Whoever was inside it could see him. How long had they been there? Had they seen what he'd done?

As if in answer, the interior light of the black SUV flicked off and on in a repeating pattern, almost as if it were trying to communicate with him through morse code.

They saw me slam the door shut, Frankie thought, his mind racing wildly. *They saw me lock the Detectives in the mines.* Whoever was within the SUV was toying with him. Messing with him. They knew.

Frankie tried to get a look at the person in the driver's seat, but the SUV's windows were tinted— only the faint glare of the interior light was visible, flicking on and off as if in laughter. Mocking him.

In a panic, Frankie threw his car into gear and pulled onto the main road, driving as fast as the engine allowed. He sped across the dark, desert night. He made it back to the main road, which stretched out before him like years in a life lived with regret. Frankie knew he would carry this moment with him forever. He wished he could undo the decision he'd made, but now, there was only one direction in which he could move— forward.

The person in that SUV knew what he had done. And somehow, Frankie could feel— deep in his bones that shivered against the desert's chill— that he would never live another day in peace again.

CHAPTER TWENTY

ACCORDING TO ETHAN'S WATCH, Annie and Ethan had only been trapped in the mines for an hour.

But— beneath the dusty scent of stale air— Ethan couldn't help but think that it felt as if they'd been trapped for days. Ethan paced in place, dirt kicking up in his wake. Nearby, Annie sat on a rock, completely calm.

"We've tried brute force— no luck there," Ethan said aloud, moving down the list of ideas for escape. "No cell service. Tell me your brilliant mind has another route?"

"I'm sure it will sort itself out!" Annie said cheerfully. She was sitting nearby on a boulder as if she were waiting for tea.

Ethan's foot caught on an unseen rock, and he stumbled, hand shooting out to the damp wall of the mine for support. Dust motes danced in the thin beam of his flashlight as it flickered—once, twice—then dimmed to a dying glow.

"Annie," he said, urgency sharpening his voice. "The light."

"If the light goes out our eyes will just have to adust to the dark I suppose," Annie's tone was light, almost playful in the oppressive darkness. "We're not doomed, Ethan. Just temporarily inconvenienced."

"Temporarily inconvenienced?" He echoed her words with a huff, trying to keep the edge of panic at bay. "You call being trapped in a mine 'temporarily inconvenienced'?"

"Semantics," she replied, brushing off his concern with a chuckle that reverberated against the cold stone walls.

Ethan shouldn't have been surprised at Annie's reaction. He had seen her in the worst of situations— under gun fire, threatened by murderers— and yet, the only time Annie felt fear was in her dreams. When she dreamt of her brother and his death— that was the only time Annie seemed to feel afraid.

With a resigned sigh, Ethan extracted the batteries from the flashlight and rubbed them vigorously against his pants. Sparks of static clung to the fabric, a faint glimmer of hope. He reinserted the batteries, gave the flashlight a shake, and pressed the power button.

Light sputtered to life, casting long shadows across the rocky expanse. Ethan released a breath he hadn't realized he'd been holding.

"Nice trick," Annie commended, peering into the depths illuminated by the renewed beam.

"Old FBI fieldwork hack," Ethan admitted, attempting nonchalance despite the adrenaline still pumping through him.

"Guess we're not completely in the dark with you around," she quipped, smiling with a confidence that belied the uncertainty of their situation.

"You knew someone was tailing us, didn't you?"

"Call it intuition," Annie shrugged, her eyes scanning the shadows as if expecting them to give up their secrets. "I'm hoping my second suspicion— that rescue is on the way— turns out to be correct as well. But it requires belief in the goodness of people, deep down underneath their lies."

"Oh no," Ethan groaned, leaning against the wall and rubbing his eyes with a weary hand. "You think we're going to rescued because people are good?" He sighed, the weight of the world on his shoulders. "Guess we're dying in here. It's been nice knowing you, Hudson."

"I happen to believe in the things I can't see," Annie shrugged. Ethan sat down next to her, taking her hand in his own. "Unlike someone *else* I know."

"This is it?" Ethan said. "I'm going to starve to death in a dark mine because you're making a point about aliens, or belief in the unknown, or—"

"You think I'm that petty?"

"You could have told me you knew someone was tailing us," Ethan offered.

"Yes," Annie agreed. "I should have told you. But I'm not sure it would have changed anything."

Ethan tried to contain his frustration. Annie was different than almost anyone he'd ever met. Her mind didn't work the same way his did. And he'd learned to trust her brilliance. But now, in the darkness of the mine, he wished she would have told him what she knew.

"Is it that you don't trust me?" he said, leaning his head against the cave wall. Annie's hand felt small within his own.

"That's not it," Annie said. "I just can't give what I don't have. It's like there's an infinite number of possible threads I'm following and any one of them could end up being true. I didn't *know* we'd get locked in the mine, although I *did* suspect we were being tailed. It takes time for suspicions to become facts and if I share my suspicions before I'm ready, I might unintentionally *create* an outcome."

Ethan shook his head, unable to believe Annie's logic. It almost sounded like superstition. Still, she had never let him down before. He held her hand up to his lips and kissed it, realizing that— if he was going to die— at least it would be next to someone he loved.

Just then, the grinding of metal on stone cut through the silence of the mines, a sound both alarming and promising.

Annie and Ethan snapped their heads toward the noise, hands instinctively reaching for nonexistent weapons.

"About time!" Annie's voice sliced the tension as the door creaked open, revealing Bianca's pink hair, glowing like a beacon in the dim light, and Harlan's bearded silhouette looming behind her. Giselle stood next to them, gun drawn, clothed head-to-toe in pajamas.

"Miss us?" Bianca chirped, brandishing a crowbar with an exuberant flourish.

"Like a hole in the head," Ethan shot back, relief evident despite his dry tone.

"Figured you needed the cavalry." Harlan's chest puffed out with pride as he presented two LED flashlights, beams piercing the murky depths.

"Or just a better locksmith," Annie said, accepting the offered light.

"Black SUV was on your tail," Bianca explained, pointing behind them with a thumb as she led the way out. "So we got Giselle and followed the follower.

"Great, a parade." Ethan rolled his eyes. He stood, helping Annie up, eager to escape the stale air that surrounded him.

"Is there anyone else in here?" Giselle asked, scanning the mines behind them for suspects. "Did you see who locked you inside."

"No," Annie answered. "Whoever locked us in here is long gone."

"Let's get out before they come back," Bianca said, shivering. "This place gives me the creeps."

The group staggered past the metal door and away from the jaws of the mines, which were wide open in protest. Together, they made their way toward the entrance. Ethan took a deep breath of crisp, clean air as the reached the desert,.

"Next time, bring snacks," Ethan suggested drily, stepping

into the open landscape, the desert sky enormous and star-studded above them.

"Your truck's still here," Bianca pointed out, a note of surprise in her voice as if vehicles frequently sprouted legs and walked off in these parts.

"Small miracles," Annie said, her brows raised in mock amazement. She ran to the back of the truck and opened up the case of bottled water she'd insisted they pack, tossing one to each member of their party. Ethan cracked the lid off of his and chugged it, downing the water as if he'd been trapped for weeks. He wiped his mouth, looking toward the road.

"Did you guys see anyone when you got here?"

"No," Bianca shook her head. "But on my way here I saw the Black SUV tailing you."

"I ran the plates as we drove this way," Giselle offered, "and Harlan was right. They're fake plates. The SUV is a ghost. Obviously someone that doesn't want to be found."

"Wait..." Harlan held up a hand, squinting into the darkness. The faint sound of an engine hummed in the distance. "Look," he whispered as headlights flickered to life across the sand, casting tubes of light toward them.

"There it is!" Harlan bounced on the balls of his feet, triumph gleaming in his eyes. "That's the one! The black SUV!"

The SUV swerved toward them. Giselle's mouth dropped open in shock. Annie stood in place, frozen. She glanced at Ethan, who furrowed his brow as if he sensed something more than what he saw. Annie watched as Ethan stepped forward toward the approaching SUV.

It pulled toward them, off-roading across the sand, coming to a stop a mere ten feet away from the group. The headlights were bright— almost blinding.

Ethan stood in front of the group, opening his arms wide as if he could protect them.

The SUV's tinted windows made it impossible to see who

was inside. But whoever it was could see them— that much was a certain.

For a moment, Annie thought someone might step out of the vehicle. Instead, there was a silent stand off. Then, the SUV's tires spun in place, and it took off across the sand, disappearing into the night as if it had never been there in the first place.

"What do you think they want?" Bianca said, voice trembling.

"I don't know," Annie said, glancing at Ethan, who was still standing in place, immobilized. A strange look crossed his face, as if he had been hit over the head. Annie recognized the feeling: Ethan had a suspicion. But he wasn't sure— yet— if it would lead to a fact. "But I expect we'll soon find out."

CHAPTER TWENTY-ONE

AFTER A LONG RIDE back to the RV park, Bianca placed her pink van back in its rental spot. Giselle went to check on her mother while Annie and Ethan left their truck in the parking lot, and the entire troup agreed to meet again at the park's firepit to discuss what they had learned.

They walked toward the gathering place together, finding that easy friendships had formed in the midst of disaster. Annie kept pace with Bianca, who was talking so fast she sounded like she'd swallowed a police scanner. "When I saw it following you guys I knew I had to do something," Bianca said, eyes wide. "It was like something out of a spy movie. Like, intense."

Ethan walked alongside, his expression a mix of amused and skeptical. "And you saw this while...?"

"Filming! Duh!" Bianca said. She adjusted her pink hair, which was the only thing brighter than her enthusiasm. "I was shooting one of my UFO vids when I saw it. I knew it was sus, so I went and grabbed Harlan."

"One of your UFO videos?" Annie asked pointedly, smiling despite herself. "I take it to mean you caught something out there?"

"Nothing big…" Bianca said nervously.

Beside her, Harlan nodded, his beard bouncing with each step. "The Government covers up half the UFO encounters anyway," he said. "They don't want us to know what we know. They put trackers in our brains."

"Wow," Ethan said. "And all this time I thought it was caffeine keeping me up at night."

Annie glanced at him, then back to Bianca. "And you're sure the black SUV was the only car you saw?

"Who else would lock you guys in the mine?" Bianca shrugged.

When they arrived at the firepit, they were pleased to find that Giselle and Maria were already there, along with Frankie and Allen. The firepit blazed like a small sun. Annie stopped short, blinking at the unexpected gathering. Giselle's mother, Maria, sat beside her, knitting needles in hand.

"Welcome!" Frankie said, raising a beer as if he'd been at the RV park all night. His blazer and tie sat akimbo, as if he'd thrown them all on in a hurry. "Planned a little party for us all. Planned it all day. I've been busy with the— planning."

"All day?" Annie said, eyeing his hands, blackened with dirt.

Frankie shrugged, a grin plastered on his face. "Charcoal dust. From the fire."

Ethan leaned in, his voice low. "Interesting timing."

As they took their seats, Allen bustled over with a tray of snacks. "UFO s'mores!" he announced, handing out graham crackers cut in the shape of flying saucers. His apron spotless and his smile wide.

"Grab a drink," Giselle called, her tone dismissive. "It's a party." She pointed at a cooler filled with beer. Ethan grabbed one, a snapping sound echoing across the night as he cracked it open.

Annie scanned the group: Giselle, Maria, Bianca, Harlan, Frankie, and Allen. Her suspects, all in one place.

Annie sat quietly, her eyes moving from person to person, like she was piecing together a puzzle.

"Quite the gathering?" Ethan whispered, sitting beside her.

"It's our suspects all in one place," Annie whispered back, keeping her voice low under the music that blared from a speaker Frankie had set out. "Just hours after we find ourselves locked in a mine."

"I'm just glad to be out," Ethan said, chugging his beer like it was the last one he'd ever get. "Even if I'm surrounded by potential murderers."

Annie ignored him, her mind raced through the possibilities and what she knew so far. Giselle, the unflappable sheriff, pretending not to care but clearly hiding something. Maria, Giselle's mother, wise and unreadable, watching everything. Bianca, fidgeting with her camera, too nervous for someone with nothing to hide. Harlan, deep in conversation with Allen, gesturing wildly. And Frankie, the cheerful host— with *dirt* on his hands.

Her thoughts circled back to the SUV. She pondered the behavior of the driver. It was as if it were being driven by someone who was watching them. Perhaps not a stalker— but a guardian. Annie felt the pieces coming together, almost within reach.

"Jamal saw a UFO the night he died," Bianca said, her voice cutting through the crackle of the fire. She looked around the circle, her eyes daring anyone to challenge her. "I got it on tape. It's legit."

The group fell silent, the night pressing in around them. Stars scattered like a cosmic spill across the sky.

"Maybe the aliens had a plan," Bianca continued quietly. "Maybe they knew Jamal was going to be murdered and they wanted to help him."

"Please," Allen said, shaking his head. "If the aliens had any plan, it was to kill Jamal to keep their existence a secret."

Ethan shook his head, his expression calm but firm. "Or maybe there is no plan. Life's random. Chaotic."

Giselle smirked, raising her bottle in a mock toast. "My plan's to enjoy the party and not care."

Maria's voice was soft, a gentle contrast to the others. "When I was little, my Grandma told me she could hear the stars at night," she said, half in Spanish. "Only when the city came, did they stop hearing the hum."

Ethan leaned forward, his tone unwavering. "Meaning?"

"That many things happen in this world you can't explain," Maria said.

Bianca crossed her arms, her lips a crooked line of defiance. "I believe in aliens. And this one is going to be my best tape yet."

Ethan sighed, a hint of exasperation in his eyes. "UFOs aren't real. Life has no meaning or plan to it."

Annie watched him, a thoughtful look on her face. "I'm not so sure," she said. "I think there's a reason we were all brought together tonight. A reason that SUV followed us. And—very soon—I'll be able to tell you all."

The group looked at her, their eyes wide, mouths agap.

One by one, they glanced at each other. Annie tracked their eyes. Maria looked at Giselle, who stared at the sandy earth. Then, Giselle glanced at Allen, who stared back at her before shifting his gaze to Bianca, who chose instead to focus on her cell phone. Harlan looked up at the stars like he was wishing for something, and— by his side— Frankie played with his tie, pinning back into place.

"That's a nice idea, Annie," Harlan broke the silence. "Whatever you say happened— even if it sounds crazy— I promise you this… I'll believe you."

His words hung in the air, a challenge, a promise. The fire snapped and hissed. Annie stood, sensing she'd overstayed her welcome. Ethan joined her, and after some polite "goodnights" they made their way back to the RV.

Annie knew they were close— so close— to the truth. She only had to tie up a few loose ends, some of which were seated around the very firepit she'd just left.

CHAPTER TWENTY-TWO

THE NEXT MORNING, Annie stood outside her RV, her phone pressed to one ear and her finger jammed in the other to block out the sound of the desert wind. The smell of charcoal lingered from the previous night's campfire, mixing with the dry air and dust. Milo's voice crackled through the line, his excitement barely contained as he told her what she'd been hoping to hear:

Russel's compound was in the mines.

"The sensor Ethan placed is a beauty," Milo said, the connection buzzing. "I'm rendering a 3D image as we speak."

"What's it show?" Annie asked, pacing. Her eyes scanned the empty RV park, the dim shapes of other RVs scattered like sleeping giants.

"I'm getting a clear structure," he replied. "About 1,000 square feet. Strong tech signature coming off it."

Annie felt a jolt of triumph. "Tech like that means it's definitely Russel's," she said. "We're close."

"I'm telling you," Milo continued, his voice a mix of glee and static, "it's running hot."

Annie's mind raced, linking this new information to

everything else they knew. The compound was real. They were on the right track. She felt a rush of determination. "What about the black SUV?" she asked, shifting the subject.

Milo paused. "Couldn't track it after it left you guys," he said. "Rejected the satellite ping. Even when I tried to get an image, the video from the satellite went dark. I've never seen anything like it."

Annie's heart sank a little. "Satellite blocking tech? Does that *exist*?"

"I guess it must," Milo confirmed. "Whoever's in that van is no joke. If they have access to technology I don't even know about they must be untouchable."

The information settled over her, heavy and significant. It meant they were dealing with a powerful organization, one with resources and reach. "Thanks, Milo," she said. "Keep researching the satellite blockage. Let me know the second you have more."

"Will do," Milo said. "Stay sharp, Annie."

She ended the call and stood for a moment, letting the desert night wrap around her. The stakes were rising. She felt the thrill of it, mixed with a familiar urgency. She turned and headed back into the RV, ready to bring Ethan up to speed. But when she entered, she found him still asleep— just as she'd left him.

Ethan lay on the lofted bed inside the RV, his arms folded behind his head. He heard the door open and close, felt the shift in the small space as Annie climbed up to join him. She curled into his side, and he welcomed her warmth.

"Stars are gone," Ethan said, gesturing to the small window. "Almost feels peaceful."

Annie settled in closer. "Milo confirmed it," she said. "Russel's compound is in the mines."

He let out a long breath, his face a mix of relief and something else. "So we're close."

She nodded, watching his expression closely. "What is it?"

Ethan hesitated, his eyes fixed on the night sky. "I want confirmation my sister is dead," he said finally. "Once and for all."

Annie felt the weight of his words, the history behind them. His need for closure was something she understood deeply. "And what if we can never get that?" she asked.

"Then I've wasted years hoping for something that's not real," Ethan said. He paused, the silence heavy. "A piece of me has always wondered if she could still be out there somewhere. I need closure. No more years wasted wondering…"

Annie listened, her empathy for him deeper than she let show. "That's not wasting years," she said softly.

He shook his head, a wry smile on his lips. "Believing she's still out there is like believing in UFOs," he said. "It's just hope over reality."

Annie looked at him, her eyes searching his. "I don't know," she said. "I'm not so sure. Maybe it's just knowing you don't have all the facts— and hoping for the best outcome of your suspicions."

The words hung between them, carrying unspoken possibilities. Annie's mind raced with everything they knew, everything they still didn't. She felt Ethan's arm tighten around her, sensing that he needed her more than she needed him.

"If your sister was alive," Annie asked quietly, "would you even *want* to know?"

Ethan didn't answer right away. His eyes stayed fixed out the window, and she felt the tension in him. "I'm not sure," he said finally, his voice almost a whisper.

They lay together in the small space, the question lingering, the desert stretching out around them. Annie felt his heartbeat against her cheek, steady but uncertain. She held him a little closer, both of them caught between hope and what came next.

"It'll be alright," Annie said. "Today, we get answers."

"Where are we starting?" Ethan asked.

Annie smiled. "Where we began. With a visit to the Sheriff."

CHAPTER TWENTY-THREE

THE SHERIFF'S office of Rachel, Nevada was a joke. A single-room shack on the edge of town, it looked like it might collapse if the wind blew too hard. Annie and Ethan exchanged a glance as they stepped inside, the bare walls and dusty floor the only witnesses to their arrival. A lone desk sat in the middle, papers scattered like it had given up on ever being organized.

"This is it?" Ethan whispered, taking in the sorry state of the place.

Annie nodded, her eyes already scanning the room for Giselle. "Given what we know about Rachel, how are you still surprised?" she whispered with a hint of irony.

Giselle stood behind the desk, her dark hair pulled back in a severe bun. She wore her uniform like it was armor, her expression as unyielding as the desert outside. Annie couldn't help but notice all the warmth they'd created between them in the evening prior was gone. Today, Giselle was all business.

"I need to talk to you about Jamal's murder."

Giselle's eyes flickered, just for a moment, before settling back into a steady glare. "I've already told you everything I know."

Annie's gaze was unrelenting. "But this time, I need you to be honest."

Giselle crossed her arms, her stance defensive. "You accusing me of something?"

Ethan stepped in, his tone soothing. "We're just trying to understand what happened. Giselle, it's clear you're not a bad person. We both recognize honorable law enforcement when we see it. Whatever you're into, we'll try to make sure you come out of it as clean as possible."

She looked between them, her resolve starting to show cracks. "There's no way out of this. No way where my life isn't over…"

Annie leaned in, her voice a mix of empathy and insistence. "You don't know that. Let us help you. If you think you can live with this secret, you're wrong. You're going to do the right thing anyway, at some point. Might be today. Might be ten years from now. But at some point— you're going to tell the truth."

Giselle's eyes darted to the floor, then back to Annie. "Why's that?"

"Because Jamal was your friend," Annie said, her words precise, cutting through Giselle's defenses. "And you're not a person who leaves a friend behind. You proved that last night."

Giselle's shoulders slumped, the fight going out of her. The weight of the dusty room seemed to settle on her as she sat down heavily in a chair. Annie watched her, sensing the shift. Ethan stayed quiet, letting Annie's strategy play out.

"I can't," Giselle said finally, her voice cracking like the ceiling above them might. Her eyes watered as she held back tears. "You don't understand. It could cost me everything."

Annie and Ethan exchanged a look, knowing they were getting close. The truth was in there, buried beneath Giselle's fear. All they had to do was dig it out.

They pulled two chairs away from the far wall and positioned them next to Giselle, surrounding her just as they had around the campfire.

Giselle's resolve crumbled like the plaster on the office walls. She looked away, unable to meet their gaze. The room was silent except for the sound of her breathing, each breath a struggle between fear and the need to confess.

"Jamal was a friend," she said, her voice breaking. "But I can't say anything without a promise from you. A deal."

"We can't cut any official deals, but you'll have to take it on faith that we're going to do everything we can to help you when this all shakes out," Ethan said. "You know enough about us now. You're going to have trust."

Annie watched her, seeing the emotional conflict writ large on her face. She recognized in Giselle the desire to help people. Generally, a person didn't go into law enforcement without it.

"You became a Sheriff to help the people of Rachel," Annie said. "Now, it's Jamal who needs you to be brave. You have to bring him to justice."

Giselle wiped her eyes with the back of her hand, her defenses gone. "I want to help," she said, her voice barely above a whisper. "But if I do, my Mom—" She stopped, the words catching in her throat.

Annie leaned forward, her voice gentle but insistent. "What about your Mom?"

Giselle took a deep breath, trying to steady herself. "She's here undocumented. The person who killed Jamal knows it. If I say anything, they'll turn her in. She'll be deported."

The weight of her words hung in the air, heavy and oppressive. Annie and Ethan exchanged a glance, both understanding the stakes. Giselle had shared a heavy secret, and she looked lighter for it.

Ethan spoke first, his tone reassuring. "We can help you with that. There are ways to protect her."

Giselle looked at him, her eyes full of doubt and desperation. "How? You're FBI, not immigration."

Annie's voice was firm, cutting through Giselle's fear. "We have connections. But we need your trust. We need you to tell us what you know."

Giselle shook her head, her fear palpable. "I can't risk it. You don't understand."

Annie's eyes were steady on hers, unwavering. "We understand more than you think."

Giselle looked down at her hands, her fingers twisting nervously. The struggle was clear, a battle between her loyalty to her family and her desire for justice for Jamal. Annie and Ethan waited, giving her the space she needed, knowing the decision had to come from her.

"My Mom," Giselle said finally, her voice a mix of resolve and resignation. "She's all I have."

Annie nodded, her expression softening. "And Jamal was all someone else had. You can help us make this right."

Ethan leaned forward, his expression earnest. "We can work with immigration, get her status protected while the investigation is ongoing. It's not easy, but it's possible."

Giselle studied them, searching for any sign of deception. "You're sure?" she asked, her voice small and uncertain.

Annie nodded, her eyes steady. "The best way to keep her safe is to cooperate with us. The more we know, the better we can protect her."

Giselle's doubt was evident, but so was her desperation. She wanted to believe them, needed to. "What if you're wrong?"

Ethan's voice was gentle, but with an underlying strength. "We're not wrong. We know what we're doing."

"We have a plan to confront the murderer," Annie said, smiling. "But we'll need your help. And you'll have to issue a signed statement with your testimony."

Giselle looked between them, her fear slowly giving way

to cautious hope. "The truth?" Giselle said, her voice a mix of relief and anxiety.

Annie nodded.

"I'll do it," Giselle relented.

Annie allowed herself an exhale, knowing how much this decision had cost Giselle. "We need to get everyone together at Alien Eats," she said, shifting into planning mode. "I want to issue my findings with all the suspects in one place."

Giselle wiped her eyes, her determination returning. "You want me to round them up?"

"Yes," Annie said. "And we'll need backup from other law enforcement. Just in case our murder tries to make a run for it."

Ethan nodded, backing her up. "Giselle, can you put a call into Vegas? Get some extra hands out here?"

Giselle took a deep breath, the weight of her secret now shared. "I can do that," she said, her voice stronger. "I'll get them all there."

Annie watched her, seeing the transformation her eyes. She had gone from frightened, to heroic. The truth tended to do that to people. "Thank you," she said, knowing how much it meant. "We won't let you down."

Giselle stood, a hint of determination in her eyes that wasn't there before. "I hope not," she said, her tone still carrying a trace of doubt but now laced with trust.

Annie and Ethan rose to leave, the dust of the office swirling around them like a cloud of uncertainty that was slowly starting to settle. They knew what needed to be done, and with Giselle's cooperation, they were one step closer to the truth. After handshakes and promises, Annie and Ethan made their exit.

Giselle watched them go, the dusty room behind her now a place of power rather than fear. She knew the risks, but she also knew her Mother would be proud of decision. She picked up the phone, ready to set the plan in motion.

"This is Sheriff Giselle calling from Rachel," she said into the line, which was connected to the Las Vegas Police Department. "I've got a sting happening and I'm 'gonna need backup."

She gulped, hoping the Vegas Police wouldn't let her down. As far as that backup went… Giselle had a feeling they were going to need it.

CHAPTER TWENTY-FOUR

IT WAS mid-afternoon when Annie gathered with all the suspects of her investigation at Alien Eats.

They sat together like a jury, the long table stretching between them— the suspects on one side, and Annie and Ethan on the other. Stars hung from the ceiling of Alien Eats, and a giant UFO sculpture loomed outside. It was a lot to take in— not unlike the news Annie was about to deliver.

Giselle wore her sheriff's uniform, her expression as rigid as her posture. Next to her, Maria whispered half in Spanish, half in English, her wise old eyes darting between faces. Bianca fiddled with a video camera, her dyed pink hair bright against the diner's green booth. Harlan nursed a cup of coffee, glancing nervously out the window. Frankie sat in a tie, though it didn't match his sweatpants. A stack of documents was piled beside him like a makeshift shield. He had taken a few hours earlier that day and printed some false legal documents in case he needed a defense— Frankie couldn't afford a lawyer, of course, but he hoped the fraudulent papers would at least slow the process down.

Annie and Ethan sat across from them, a picture of professional calm amidst the chaos. Annie's sharp eyes surveyed the group, while Ethan's broad-shouldered frame leaned forward, approachable but firm. Allen, in his white apron, circled the table, refilling drinks and dropping off dishes as if this gathering were a family reunion and not a murder investigation.

"So," Harlan said, breaking the silence with his sandpaper tone. "Why are we here?"

Annie let the pause hang, her fingers tapping a silent rhythm on the table. "We know who killed Jamal."

The group gasped in unison as if the air had been sucked out of a room. Even the paper stars overhead seemed to tremble.

"That's right," Annie continued, her voice precise and steady. "But to get to the truth, we'll need to go person by person."

Bianca crossed her arms, her eyes narrowing. "What do you mean?"

"I mean," Annie said. "That each and every person at this table has a secret. To be fair, I'll start with us," Annie said, nodding toward Ethan. "Two outsiders who happen to come to town at the same time as that a murder occurs. Suspicious, don't you think?"

"I'll say," Harlan agreed, nodding heartily.

Annie paused, drawing them in, letting the silence work its magic. "We came to town because a man named Russel Grey was connected to the death of both our siblings, who were murdered when we were teenagers. That's how Ethan and I— connected. We were both affected by a terrible crime committed by a serial killer known as the Real Estate Ripper."

The room went still, the only sound the clink of Allen's coffee pot as he refilled Harlan's cup, hovering nearby so as not to miss a word. Maria crossed herself, whispering for divine protection. Giselle's lips pressed into a thin, tight line. Frankie shook his head, muttering something that sounded like "Oh boy." Bianca lowered her camera, stunned, while Harlan let out a low whistle, his eyes narrowing with interest.

"This is... wow," Bianca finally said. "Like, I didn't see that coming."

Annie nodded, letting them absorb the shock. "In pursuing the Real Estate Ripper, we stumbled on a man named Russel Grey, who was connected to a dangerous group called 'The Collective.'"

Harlan's eyes lit up with the fervor of a true believer. "I knew it! I've been trying to tell everyone about this for years!"

Ethan raised an eyebrow, amused. "Is that so?"

Harlan leaned forward, the intensity of a man vindicated. "Shadow organization. Real secretive. Real dangerous. There's all kinds of Reddit threads about in the Conspiracy forum. You're sayin' Russel was part of it?"

"That's exactly what we're saying," Annie replied. "Sadly, Russel was murdered before he could tell us anything. But he led us here, where he claimed to have a secret compound that would help us bring down The Collective."

Frankie's face went pale, the color of unsold pancakes. "A secret compound here in Rachel?"

"Maybe," Annie said, her voice a needle pricking the tension. "But before we'd even had a chance to look for it, we stumbled on Jamal's murder, and found we had yet another case to solve. Which brings us to all of *you*." Annie held her arms open as if she were introducing contestants at a beauty pageant. "Let's start with... *Bianca*."

All eyes turned to the young woman, the room's pressure shifting like a spotlight. She looked at Annie, a mix of fear and defiance in her eyes.

"Bianca," Annie continued, her tone as sharp as her gaze. "You're a successful YouTuber, renowned for your work documenting alien phenomena."

Bianca blinked, unsure if this was praise or a trap. "Uh, yeah. That's me."

"You've earned quite a following," Annie went on, her

words deliberate, precise. "But after watching your videos online, I couldn't help but wonder..."

Bianca swallowed hard, her face losing its color, her hair now the brightest thing about her. "Wonder what?"

"...if you might be fabricating much of your content."

The accusation hung in the air, as heavy and tangible as the UFO outside. The group watched Bianca, waiting for her response, the room's silence as thick as the diner's milkshakes.

"Okay," she said, her voice small but determined. "What Annie told you is true."

The group leaned in, drawn by the drama of their only local celebrity.

"I've been faking my videos," she confessed, her words tumbling out. "But only because I want to capture something real. I mean, *really* real. Not like those other hoaxers."

Annie's eyes stayed on her, reading every flicker of emotion. "That's why you stationed cameras all around town?"

"Yeah," Bianca said, her voice gaining strength. "And they were rolling the night Jamal was killed."

Giselle's eyes widened in shock. "Bianca! You've had footage of the murderer all this time?"

Bianca nodded. She reached into her backpack and pulled out a harddrive, which she slid across the table to Annie.

"After we rescued you from the mines last night and we all sat around the firepit, I realized I had to come clean," Bianca said, looking down at the table. "All that talk about aliens and the stars... I realized there are bigger things than me at play here. I mean, my life is just one tiny experience in the great unknown. So, I was going to tell you today, but then you asked to meet so I brought it with me." She nodded at the hardrive, which was now safely in Annie's hands. "You'll see it on the video. The murderer steps out of the diner right after Jamal was killed. It's all on tape."

Annie's voice was soft but relentless. "Can you please

share with the group why you chose to hide this information?"

Bianca took a deep breath, her face a mix of shame and defiance. "The murderer threatened me. He sent me an email once he realized the cameras were there. Said he'd tell the world my videos were fake if I didn't delete it. The only problem is, he sent the email from Jamal's account. So I have no idea who did it."

Maria gasped, her hand flying to her chest. Frankie muttered "Oh boy" for the third time. Harlan's gaze darted between Bianca and Annie, trying to piece it all together. Giselle looked at her softly, a knowing pain crossing her expression.

Annie nodded, her expression almost gentle. "It seems our suspect enjoys blackmail, doesn't it?" Annie asked, glancing at Giselle before turning back to Bianca. "But like so many of you at this table, Bianca is a good person. When she saw the black van following us that night, she called Harlan and Giselle, and the three of them rescued us."

Bianca looked up, surprised by the unexpected praise. "I didn't want anything bad to happen to you guys."

Ethan cringed, rolling his eyes. "Well… we appreciate that." Annie elbower him hard, then turned her attention to Harlan.

"That brings us to Harlan, whose conspiracy theories aren't off base. He's been right about the black SUV this entire time."

Harlan puffed up, the proud owner of a finally validated worldview. "Told you all so!"

"I suspect quite strongly now that the black SUV is connected to The Collective," Annie continued, her gaze sweeping the table. "But the person who was in the black SUV wasn't the one who locked us in the van that night…"

The room went still, every pair of eyes glued to Annie, every ear straining for the next word.

"Instead," she said, drawing out the pause, "it was..."

She let the suspense build, her timing impeccable, her delivery flawless.

"Frankie."

The reaction was instant and electric, like someone had just detonated a truth bomb in the middle of the diner.

The group gasped again, a chorus of shock rippling across the table. They stared at Frankie as if he were a leper. His lanky frame seemed to shrink, his tie suddenly looking too big for his neck.

"Me?" Frankie squeaked, his voice cracking. "You think I did it?"

Annie's gaze was unyielding. "We *know* you did."

Frankie crumpled, the confession spilling out of him like air from a punctured tire. "Okay, okay! I locked you in the mines!"

Maria crossed herself for the third time that day, whispering for divine protection. Giselle's eyes widened, her stern demeanor slipping. Harlan leaned back, a satisfied grin spreading across his face.

"But I didn't mean to hurt you," Frankie blurted, his voice desperate. "I just... I panicked."

Annie tilted her head, her expression a mix of curiosity and mild amusement. "Why don't you tell us what you were so afraid of?"

Frankie's shoulders sagged, the weight of his secret finally too much to bear. "I don't own the land the RV park is on. It's government land, and I'm not supposed to be using it. My Grandma didn't own it either. We've been renting out spots we're not allowed to use. Basically, all of you are unknowing squatters, paying *me* to live on Government land I don't even own. They could kick us off at any time."

The confession hung in the air, absurd and tragic and a little bit funny. The group stared at him, trying to process this bizarre twist. Then, shouts echoed across the table. Harlan stood, splashing his soda over Frankie's suit.

"You *idiot!*" Harlan shouted.

Bianca leaned over the table, pointing a finger at Frankie. "And to think you've been charging me double!"

"*Estúpido!*" Maria exclaimed.

Ethan put his fingers in his mouth, whistling loudly to bring the group back to Earth. "Let's give Frankie a chance to explain," Ethan suggested.

"Oh boy," Frankie said, shaking his head. "I'm gonna be in so much trouble."

Ethan leaned forward, his tone gentle but firm. "You locked us in the mines because you thought we'd find out?"

"It was the look on Annie's face! The way she stared at the fake land deed I gave you. It seemed like she already knew. You have to understand, my Grandma started the scam a long time ago and never got found out. I didn't want to be the one to ruin it all. The RV park is all I have." Frankie's eyes were wide with panic. "I was gonna let you out, I swear! But then I saw that black SUV watching, and I freaked."

Annie nodded, her expression softening. "And you regretted it as soon as it was over."

Frankie nodded, his face a picture of guilty relief. "I'm real sorry, Annie. Ethan."

"Apology *not* accepted, Frankie," Ethan said, still seething. "But we'll get to that later."

Annie's voice was almost kind. "We understand you, Frankie."

The tension in the room ebbed, the drama deflating. But Annie's next words sent it soaring back to life.

"Besides... you and Bianca weren't the only ones with a secret."

Her eyes landed on Giselle, the focus shifting with the precision of a well-timed plot twist. Giselle sat rigidly, her mother's hand on her arm, the group's anticipation building around her like a storm.

The group watched Giselle, their anticipation thick enough to cut with a knife. Maria's hand was on her daughter's arm, squeezing gently, urging her to speak. Giselle's eyes were fixed on the table.

"Giselle," Maria said softly. "Tell them the truth. *La verdad.*"

The Sheriff looked up, her eyes meeting Annie's. They were full of conflict, of fear, of something more than just a secret.

"I saw him," Giselle said, her voice breaking the tension like a sudden clap of thunder. "I saw the murderer standing over Jamal's body."

The group's reaction was explosive, a burst of sound and motion. Bianca's camera whirred to life. Harlan's coffee sloshed over the rim of his cup. Frankie looked like he'd just been handed a life sentence. Ethan's eyes met Annie's, a silent exchange of understanding.

"But he didn't want me to tell on him," Giselle continued, her voice growing stronger, more resolute. "He threatened me just like he threatened Bianca."

Annie leaned in, her attention as focused as a laser beam. "What kind of threat?"

Giselle's eyes flicked to her mother, then back to the group. "He said he'd have my mom deported if I told the truth."

The group sat in stunned silence, the full weight of the revelation settling over them like a heavy fog. Maria patted her daughter on the back, proud she'd made the choice to tell the truth.

Frankie was the first to break it, her voice urgent and demanding. "Who? Who was it?"

Giselle's eyes found Allen, who was standing in the kitchen, just visible through a cutout across the bar. Just then, as if he knew he'd been summoned, Allen crossed the diner, bringing a pot of coffee with him. He stood beside Harlan, refilling his mug.

"Anyone else?" Allen asked, doing his best to seem as if nothing was wrong.

Shaking, Giselle stood and pointed at him, her voice steady and clear. "It was Allen. *Allen* killed Jamal."

The moment stretched like a rubber band, ready to snap. Then Annie felt the jolt, the spark of danger, the instant before it hit. Allen turned the mug of hot coffee he was holding toward her, splashing it onto her torso. The coffee spread across the table, scalding hot, a liquid explosion aimed right at her. She jerked back, the steaming brew barely missing her, splattering across the UFO-themed tablecloth.

Allen ran, his apron flapping behind him like a white flag of surrender. But there was no surrender in his eyes, only panic and determination.

"Stop him!" Ethan shouted, leaping to his feet.

The group erupted into chaos, chairs scraping, voices shouting, the sound an overwhelming, dissonant chorus. Frankie stumbled in his haste, nearly tripping over Bianca's outstretched leg. Harlan made a grab for Allen's arm but caught only air. Giselle was on her feet, her training kicking in, her badge flashing as she moved to block Allen's path.

But Allen was fast— faster than any of them expected. He ducked under Giselle's reach, a nimble twist that took him past Maria, past Harlan, past the shocked and scrambling group.

He was almost to the door.

The group stood frozen, the reality of his escape sinking in.

But if they'd taken a moment to look over their shoulders, they would have noticed Annie, still seated at the table, a small smile playing on the corner of her lips.

CHAPTER TWENTY-FIVE

ALLEN'S EYES darted to the door of Alien Eats. Freedom was one sprint away, if he could just make it. He was at the front door, and the handle was in his grasp. He opened it wide, glancing at the— *"It's out of this world!"*— neon sign above the alien statue in the parking lot. Just a few more steps and he'd be—

He skidded to a stop. The diner was surrounded. Cops everywhere. His mouth went dry. A wall of blue uniforms blocked the exit, guns drawn. They pushed him backward into the diner, swarming toward him. "Police! Stay where you are!" they shouted, voices overlapping. Allen's mind raced. He was screwed. Totally screwed. He spun around, hoping for another way out, but his legs were leaden. He made it two steps toward the kitchen before he heard the pounding of feet behind him.

They were on him in seconds. "Get down! Get down!" Allen's world tilted. He stumbled, trying to get away, but the sound of shouts and chairs scraping filled his ears.

Allen hit the linoleum hard. Pain shot through his shoulder as the Police tackled him, pinning him down. His cheek pressed against the sticky floor, right next to a piece of gum. "I'm innocent! I didn't do anything!" It felt like a hundred hands were on him, grabbing, holding, twisting his arms behind his back. He tried to squirm free, but the more he struggled, the tighter they held him.

Giselle's figure loomed over him. He recognized her by her boots. "I'd like to do the honors, boys," she said, leaning down to Allen's level as a cop slammed handcuffs on his wrists. "Allen, you're under arrest. You have the right to remain silent. Anything you say can and *will* be used against you— you have the right to an attorney." Giselle bent down lower and whispered viciously in his ear, "You thought you *had* me, but what you didn't know is that I wasn't working alone."

Allen's mind was a blur. He couldn't believe it. Couldn't believe they'd caught him. "You have no idea!" he shouted, voice cracking with frustration. The cops hauled him to his feet, dragging him toward the door. "I did everything right! Everything! Got the degree. Worked my ass off to get somewhere. And what do I get? Nothing!" He was almost in tears, his words echoing off the alien-themed walls.

Allen's legs barely worked as they shoved him outside, his shoes slipping on the floor. "I did everything right!" he yelled again, a desperate, final cry.

"Bye, Allen," Bianca waved cheerfully. She held her camera in the air, recording every moment. "I can't wait to make this guy famous on YouTube," she said to Giselle, smiling.

Allen's voice faded into the distance as the door swung shut behind him, leaving the remaining suspects to their gossip and the blinking neon sign. Now that the chaos had settled, an eerie calm remained.

"Should we return to our lunch?" Annie asked.

One by one, the group returned to their seats. Annie took another sip of her coffee, clearing her throat before continuing her story as if nothing unusual had happened. "So, you see,

Jamal was murdered by Allen, who had recently earned a degree, but was unable to find a job. Frustrated by his lack of opportunity, he modified Jamal's will to leave himself the diner, then ended the life of the very man who had given him his first opportunity. Allen left the fake will in an obvious spot in Jamal's office. We found the original will in Allen's RV, which we searched earlier this morning," Annie added. "It seems Frankie isn't the only person in town who enjoys creating fraudulent paperwork."

Frankie flushed.

Ethan leaned across the table, eyes wide with curiosity. "And what about the UFO Jamal saw before he died?" he asked, his voice a mix of disbelief and intrigue. The diner was quieter now, the chaos of the arrest fading into the past. The alien decor seemed to lean in, listening. "Was it an illusion… or a trick? Some kind of distraction Allen made to take the focus off of himself as a suspect? Who faked that, and why?"

Annie took a sip of coffee, her expression unreadable. "The UFO was real," she said with a casual shrug. "The simplest explanation is often the right one. The UFO was an actual unidentified object, maybe from another world."

Ethan blinked, his mind trying to catch up with her words. He looked like she'd just told him the earth was flat. "You're serious?" he said, his voice catching on a laugh. "That's your answer?"

Annie set the cup down, eyes meeting his with calm certainty. "Why not?" she said. Her tone was so matter-of-fact, it was almost funny. "Everything else fits. Jamal saw what he saw. We're in Rachel, which is known for alien sightings. Given the available facts, it almost seems ridiculous *not* to reach the conclusion the UFO is real."

"Gotcha," Bianca smiled at Ethan, recording his reaction to this shocking news. "I'm going to title this video, 'Non-believer gets schooled.'"

Ethan sat back, running a hand through his hair. "I can't

believe this. You, of all people. The great Annie Hudson, private investigator, mystery-solver extraordinaire, and you're telling me it was *aliens*?"

She leaned forward, her gaze steady. "Think about it, Ethan. Harlan saw the UFO, too. Bianca has the object on tape. We both watched the footage and— even with our knowledge of government programs, we both have to admit — there's no object in existence that can move like that. And as Bianca pointed out, even congress believes in aliens now."

"Yeah, Ethan, get with the times!" Bianca laughed.

Ethan shook his head, trying to wrap his mind around it. The idea was so... simple, but so challenging. "But you're the one who always says we have to follow facts," he said, a grin tugging at the corners of his mouth. "And now you're going full X-Files on me?"

Annie's lips curved in the slightest hint of a smile. "Sometimes the truth is stranger than fiction."

"I don't know whether to laugh or start believing," he said, watching her with a mix of admiration and bewilderment. "You're really sticking to this, aren't you?"

Annie nodded, her eyes twinkling with a rare glimpse of humor. "Until proven otherwise," she said, her voice firm but playful. "You've got to keep an open mind, Ethan." Then, she added sadly. "You're going to need it, I'm afraid. We're not done with the surprises yet."

Ethan couldn't help but laugh, shaking his head in defeat. "Fine, you win," he said, raising his hands in surrender. "But I reserve the right to say 'I told you so' when little green men don't show up."

Annie leaned back, satisfied. "Deal," she said, picking up her coffee again.

The stars on the ceiling seemed to wink at them, silent witnesses to the mystery that might just be out of this world.

Bianca's eyes were wide with excitement as she turned her

camera off and set it down for the first time all day. "I caught it all on tape," she said, practically bouncing in her seat. Her pink hair bobbed with every word. "The murder being solved. And a real UFO! I'm gonna post the truth online. It's gonna blow up."

Ethan watched her, amused by her energy. Suddenly, he sat up, bothered by something that had only just occurred to him. "And what about the black SUV?" he asked, his tone shifting to curiosity.

"Yeah," Harlan said, almost offended his pet project had been left to the end of the explanation. "We need some resolution here. As the first person to identify the SUV, I'm ready to be proven right." Harlan practically beamed, sitting back in his chair. "So what is it, Annie? It's all connected, isn't it? The black SUV involves Aliens, the government, the Collective. One big conspiracy."

Annie interrupted, her voice cutting through Harlan's ramblings like a knife. "The black SUV is not any of those things."

"Then what is it?" Harlan asked, defensive.

"I'll have to show you," she said, quiet and serious. "But it seems I've been offered some help." Annie nodded toward the window next to the booth, looking at something in the diner's parking lot. Everyone turned, staring at the black SUV, parked harmlessly facing the diner. The windows retained their tint, making it impossible to discern the figure within. But it was clear the person inside the SUV saw them: the headlights flashed once, then twice, almost as if the SUV was urging them forward.

"What on Earth… ?" Ethan said. His heart was racing, but he wasn't sure why. Something about this moment felt defining, as if the decision he'd make in the next few minutes might determine all that was to come.

Annie turned to face Ethan, a concerned look on her face. "I need to know you can handle it," she said, putting a hand on his knee. "I need to know that you can be open-minded before we follow them."

Ethan had never seen Annie like this— she was unflappable. The concern etched across her face made him afraid. Still, he'd coming seeking the truth. And there was no turning back now.

"What could be stranger than aliens being real?" Ethan smiled.

"We'll come with you," Harlan volunteered.

"Yeah," Bianca added, "I'd like to see what happens next."

"I think Ethan and I should tackle this one alone—" Annie started to say, but Ethan shook his head.

"They can come," he told her. He picked up on a skeptical glaze to her stare. "I kind of like this group," he whispered under his breath. "Might as well have backup, right?"

Annie considered, then nodded.

"Everyone," she said, "this time it's not the SUV following us. This time— we're following *them*."

CHAPTER TWENTY-SIX

THE DRIVE WAS QUIET. An eerie stillness settled over the inside of the pickup truck as Ethan followed the black SUV across the desert sand, heading North to the open landscape that rested above the town of Rachel. Ethan glanced over at Annie, who had been silent the entire ride. Her head was resting on the window, her eyes looking out at the horizon like it was a puzzle she couldn't solve.

"They're taking us back the way we went the other night," Ethan offered unhelpfully.

"Yes they are," Annie agreed. "I figured as much. I'd like to believe they were just waiting for the right moment."

"The right moment?"

"This person has likely been observing us," Annie said, thinking aloud. "After all, they knew we were headed for the mines and followed us there. They allowed Bianca to see them in our wake—"

"They were going *so* fast!" Bianca exclaimed. She was sitting in the jump-seat between Annie and Ethan. The rest of the group was in Giselle's Sheriff cruiser, which was visible in the rearview mirror, but Bianca had insisted on joining Annie and Ethan. "I couldn't miss 'em."

Ethan clutched the steering wheel tighter, staying close on the tail of the black SUV, which was just a few meters in front of them.

"If they'd wanted to go undetected, they could have taken a different route," Annie continued. "But as Bianca just shared, the person driving the SUV made it a point to be seen. I believe they knew Frankie was up to no good, and urged others to come to our rescue. They waited outside the mines to make sure we exited safely. Because of that, I believe they mean us no harm."

"Then why not show themselves?" Ethan countered.

Annie shrugged. "Maybe they were waiting for us to solve the mystery of Jamal's death. Or," she paused, wondering if she should say what was on her mind, "Or maybe they knew we needed more time to come around to the idea."

"Annie, can you just tell it to me straight for once—"

"I don't think I can," Annie said regretfully. "If I'm wrong—"

"You're never wrong."

"I could be this time! Maybe it's not who I think it is and it's just a regular old bad guy," Annie suggested.

"You're *never* wrong," Ethan said again.

"— it would be better to let them explain—"

"I'd rather hear it from you."

"But then I'll be in the middle…"

"Guys?" Bianca interjected, disrupting an impending argument. "I think we're here." She pointed out the front window, where the black SUV had turned off the road. It trundled across the sand, struggling toward the familiar exterior of the mines.

"The mines," Ethan said, following the SUV toward the now familiar, decrepit exterior. When the SUV stopped, Ethan also put the truck in park. Giselle's Sheriff cruiser pulled up beside him, and the entire gang spilled out of the car: Giselle, Maria, and Harlan.

Bianca unlatched her seatbelt, exiting the pickup truck behind Annie and Ethan, who stood at the front of the group. Everyone waited, breathless.

Then, Ethan took a few steps forward, making his way toward the SUV. He held up a hand as if to signal they came in peace.

"How sure are you they mean us no harm, Annie?"

Behind his shoulder came the answer: "Ninety-five percent."

Ethan cringed. His life hung on the unkown five percent. Then, he felt a warm hand slide into his own. It was Annie. She turned to him, more afraid than he'd ever seen her.

"Annie?" Ethan asked, concerned. "What's—"

"Don't be mad at me," she said. "If I'm right and this is who I think it is, just don't be mad at me. I couldn't tell you if I wasn't sure. And I'm *still* not sure but on the drive here it just seemed clearer and clearer…"

Now, Ethan was *really* concerned. "Annie, what am I missing here?"

"Remember when we talked about what you would do if a spaceship landed right in front of you?"

"Yeah."

"Well, Earth to Ethan," Annie said.

Before Ethan could ask his next question, the door to the SUV opened, and a figure stepped out of the driver's side. She was wearing black combat boots, her short, asymmetrical hair pushed to one side. Her clothes were all black under a long jacket, and when she removed her sunglasses, the look of concern on her face was so earnest it made Ethan want to take a step back.

"That's her!" Harlan shouted, jumping up in the air and pointing at the woman in front of her. "That's the government agent! She's the one I saw! I was right. I *told* you all—"

"Sshhhh," Giselle said, sensing something bigger was

going on. Still, she moved a hand toward her service weapon, just in case Harlan wasn't wrong.

"You're going to have to let me explain—" the woman said, moving around the black SUV and closing the distance between them. Her hands were up in the air to signal she meant no harm.

Ethan squinted against the desert sun, sure what he was seeing was a mirage. He remembered the wanted posters from his childhood. The photograph of his sister on her first day of college. "Megan," he said, feeling as if someone had punched him. He turned to Annie, lost for words.

"I didn't think I'd be right—" Annie said, her eyes watering. Tears started to fall down her cheeks, but she ignored them. "I thought for sure I was imagining it, just wishing it would be true—"

"Hey now, what's all this?" Harlan shouted, throwing his arms up in the air. "Is she a government agent, or what?"

"No," Ethan said, still barely able to breath. His voice sounded far away, like it belonged to someone else. "She's... my sister."

No one in the group made a sound. The desert sun hung low in the sky. The town of Rachel wasn't a place Ethan had expected to find an alien encounter, but now, here it was— right in front of him.

And no matter what happened, Ethan knew his life would never be the same again.

MURDER IN THE HOMETOWN

To continue the adventure, look for "Murder in the Hometown," Book Six in the Private Investigator Annie Hudson Mystery series!

MORE FROM VALERIE BRANDY

The Annie Hudson Real Estate Mystery Series:

- "Murder Behind the Gates" — The Private Investigator Annie Hudson Mystery Series, Book One.
- "Murder in the Penthouse" — The Private Investigator Annie Hudson Mystery Series, Book Two.
- "Murder on the Farm" — The Private Investigator Annie Hudson Mystery Series, Book Three.
- "Murder on the Commune" — The Private Investigator Annie Hudson Mystery Series, Book Four.
- "Murder in the Desert" — The Private Investigator Annie Hudson Mystery Series, Book Five.
- "Murder in the Hometown" — The Private Investigator Annie Hudson Mystery Series, Book Six.

The Predator / Prey Thriller Series:

- "Trail of Obsession" — The Predator/ Prey Thriller Series, Book One.
- "Lies Run Deep" — The Predator/ Prey Thriller Series, Book Two.
- "The Trap is Set" — The Predator/ Prey Thriller Series, Book Three.
- "The Woman in the Wind" — The Predator/ Prey Thriller Series, Book Four.

COMING SOON:

The Rebecca Orange Cozy Castle Mystery Series

- Mystery at Monrovia Castle — Book One
- A Victim in the Village — Book Two
- A Royal Ruse — Book Three

Most books available in large print!

LETTER FROM THE AUTHOR

Dear Reader,

Thank you for dedicating your time to the world of Annie Hudson and the Real Estate Mystery series! I'm a screenwriter and filmmaker coming to books from Film & TV, but one thing I love about books in particular, is connecting directly with a community of readers. It's very special to be able to speak with you and hear what you want from characters in our novels.

I hope you'll reach out to me by joining my mailing list at the link below! I love to keep my readers updated on new releases, offer advanced copies, free giveaways of novellas, sneak previews, and more.

If you liked Annie Hudson, I hope you'll keep reading the rest of the series, which continues to grow!

And if you want to read more from me in general, I hope you'll check out the list of my books on the previous page.

Warmly,

— Valerie Brandy

www.valeriebrandy.com